KU-251-857

THE SANTANA HEIR

BY
ELIZABETH LANE

ABERDEENSHIRE LIBRARIES	
3156998	
Bertrams	30/01/2015
ROM Pbk	£3.49

MILLS BOON

All rights reserved including the right of reproduction in whole
or in part in any form. This edition is published by arrangement with
Harlequin Books S.A.

This is a work of fiction. Names, characters, places, locations and
incidents are purely fictional and bear no relationship to any real
life individuals, living or dead, or to any actual places, business
establishments, locations, events or incidents. Any resemblance is
entirely coincidental.

This book is sold subject to the condition that it shall not, by way of
trade or otherwise, be lent, resold, hired out or otherwise circulated
without the prior consent of the publisher in any form of binding or
cover other than that in which it is published and without a similar
condition including this condition being imposed on the subsequent
purchaser.

® and TM are trademarks owned and used by the trademark owner
and/or its licensee. Trademarks marked with ® are registered with the
United Kingdom Patent Office and/or the Office for Harmonisation in
the Internal Market and in other countries.

Published in Great Britain 2014
by Mills & Boon, an imprint of Harlequin (UK) Limited,
Eton House, 18-24 Paradise Road, Richmond, Surrey, TW9 1SR

© 2014 Elizabeth Lane

ISBN: 978 0 263 90858 9

Harlequin (UK) Limited's policy is to use papers that are natural,
renewable and recyclable products and made from wood grown in
sustainable forests. The logging and manufacturing processes conform
to the legal environmental regulations of the country of origin.

Printed and bound in Spain
by Blackprint CPI, Barcelona

THE SANTANA HEIR

One

Emilio Santana stared at the folder on the massive mahogany desk—the desk that had served the head of the Santana family for seven generations. Until two weeks ago that desk had belonged to his brother. Now it was his.

He was still reeling from Arturo's death in a highway accident. But the vast Santana business holdings couldn't wait for grief. Catapulted into place as the new jefe, Emilio had a world of things to learn—and barely enough time to learn them. He'd never wanted this responsibility. But now it was his—for life.

Arturo had always been the one who took care of things. While Emilio jetted around the world, partying with rock stars and dating glamorous women, Arturo had managed the family estate in Urubamba, the corporate offices in Lima and the portfolio of global investments and properties that comprised the Santana fortune. Steady and competent, Arturo had always been there to bail his wild younger brother out of trouble. Now he was gone, the reality of his loss still sinking in.

Since the funeral and the novena, Emilio had spent much of his time going through the files in Arturo's home office. Invoices, contracts, business correspondence. It was all a lot to take in, but he'd found nothing out of the ordinary.

Until now.

The manila folder, marked "Personal," had been tucked into the back of the file drawer. Inside, Emilio found a certified envelope, addressed to Arturo and mailed from Tucson, Arizona, ten months earlier. Inside was a folded letter, printed on plain white paper and signed in a strong but feminine hand.

March 10
Dear Mr. Santana:

It saddens me to inform you that my stepsister, Cassidy Miller, passed away March 1 of this year, due to a brain tumor...

Cassidy dead? But how could that be? Emilio stared at the page in disbelief. Cassidy had been so beautiful, so full of life and mischief. A model with a reputation as a party girl, Cassidy Miller had been doing a fashion shoot in Cusco when Emilio had met her. After the shoot he'd invited her and several model friends to spend a few days at the Urubamba estate. One look at Arturo, and she'd cancelled an upcoming assignment to stay with him. During the five weeks they'd spent together, Emilio's brother had never looked happier. Then Cassidy had vanished from his life. Emilio had wondered why, but if Arturo had known, he'd never said a word.

Biting back emotion Emilio read on.

I know this news will come as a shock. Cassidy begged me not to tell you about her illness. But now that she's gone I feel duty-bound to write to you for another reason. In the last days of her life, Cassidy gave birth to a baby boy. Since he was born February 26, nine months from the time she was with you in Peru, I have every reason to believe he's your son.

Rest assured that I'm not writing to make any claim on your wealth or your estate. In fact, if you agree, I would like to raise the boy myself. Little Zac, as Cassidy named him, will be well cared for here with me. I've brought him home and would love to raise him as my own. My lawyer has advised me to inform you of his birth and ask your permission before taking steps to adopt him.

My business card is enclosed. If I don't hear from you, I'll assume you have no interest in the boy and proceed with the adoption.

Sincerely,

Grace Chandler

Emilio reread the letter. His numbness ebbed as the news sank home. Cassidy was gone forever. But Arturo had left a son—a son he'd kept secret. Why?

Looking for answers, Emilio unfolded a second sheet of paper—this one a photocopy of Arturo's reply.

March 31

Dear Miss Chandler:

My condolences on your loss. You may adopt the boy on condition that he have no future contact with the Santana family, nor any legal claim to the Santana estate. I plan to be married soon and start a family of my own. The appearance of an illegitimate son

would cause pain and embarrassment, which I wish
to avoid at all cost.

If I can trust you to understand my position and
honor my wishes, I will leave this matter entirely in
your hands.

Yours truly,

Arturo Rafael Santana y Morales

Emilio studied the letter. The language sounded brusque,
even cold. But Arturo himself had often sounded cold and
closed-off after Cassidy left. And even before she came into
his life, he had always put family interests ahead of personal feelings. At the time when he'd written the letter, he'd
become engaged to Mercedes Villanueva, the daughter of a
wealthy neighbor. The wedding had never taken place, but
Emilio could understand Arturo's not wanting an illegitimate
offspring to interfere.

Illegitimate. Such an ugly word for an innocent child.
Turning, he gazed out the window, which commanded a view
of the Santana estate. Situated in the lush Sacred Valley of
the Incas, the land had been in his family since the 1600s
when Spanish conquistador Miguel Santana had acquired it
as a royal grant. Santana had married an Inca princess and
settled into the life of a country gentleman. The land reforms
of the 1960s had trimmed away most of the original grant,
but the heart of the estate remained, as did the well-managed
Santana fortune.

The Santanas themselves hadn't fared so well. Emilio's
firstborn brother had died of a childhood illness. Now that
Arturo was gone, Emilio was the only remaining Santana
male. Unless he married and sired an heir—a prospect that
loomed like a prison sentence—the family holdings could
be fated for seizure by the government or split among his
distant kin.

Emilio reread both letters. Arturo had never wanted to father a child out of wedlock. The impulsive Cassidy must have caught him off guard, without protection. But what mattered now was that Arturo had left a son—a boy who, by now, would be almost a year old.

Legitimate or not, there was no way Emilio would turn his back on his own flesh and blood. Especially when that child could be the key to carrying on the Santana legacy. Maybe this Grace Chandler person would be amenable to some kind of arrangement. If not, he had the means to exercise his family's legal rights.

Writing or calling would only complicate matters. He would leave for Arizona tomorrow.

Tucson, Arizona

"How about some lunch, big boy?" Grace lifted Zac out of the jogging stroller and carried him into the house. At eleven months, he was getting heavy. Soon he'd be walking. Then she'd really have her hands full.

Buckling him into his high chair she washed his hands, gave him some finger food and kept an eye on him as he fed himself. Cassidy's son was a beautiful child, with ebony curls and heart-melting brown eyes. His coloring would have come from his Peruvian father. But when Grace looked at the little boy, it was Cassidy she saw looking back at her.

Ever since she had found out that Cassidy was pregnant— and that it was unlikely she would live to raise her son herself—it had been Grace's plan to adopt her stepsister's baby. The paperwork had taken months, but now the wait was almost over. In a few weeks she would finalize the process that would make Zac her legal son—the only child she could ever have.

Splat! A chunk of cooked, mashed carrot hit her cheek and stuck there. Zac grinned and giggled, showing his new baby teeth. Throwing food was his newest discovery, and he was good at it.

"That's quite an arm you've got, mister. We should think about baseball later on." Laughing, she boosted him out of the chair and untied his bib. "Time to wash up. Let's go."

Zac had managed to get as much lunch on his face and hands as in his mouth. As she passed the hallway mirror, Grace caught a glimpse of herself with the baby in her arms. The two of them looked like they'd been in a food fight. In the few seconds it had taken her to cross the small kitchen, he'd smeared the front of her white T-shirt and coated a lock of her hair. Between her morning run and Zac's meal, she was a sweaty, sticky mess. As soon as the little mischief-maker was down for his nap, she'd be ready for a shower.

Grace had just stepped into the bathroom with the baby when the front doorbell rang.

Talk about timing… It was most likely a delivery or a salesperson. Maybe if she didn't answer, the caller would give up and leave.

But the bell rang again, more insistently this time. With a sigh of surrender, Grace switched the baby to her left hip, strode to the front door and opened it.

The tall, dark man on the porch was a stranger. But Grace recognized him from his photos in the supermarket tabloids, usually with some actress or model draped on his arm. *The Peruvian Playboy,* one scandal sheet had dubbed him.

Arturo Santana's brother wouldn't just drop by to say hello. Grace's stomach knotted as she met his piercing eyes. Emilio Santana, she sensed, had come here for a reason. And that reason must have something to do with Zac.

Clasping the baby, Grace braced herself for trouble.

Emilio's gaze took in the woman and child. She was athletically built, her long, tanned legs stretching from white running shoes to black nylon shorts. Strings of dark blond hair had escaped from her sweatband to dangle around her carrot-smudged face. Wide hazel eyes—her most striking feature—blazed defiance. With her golden coloring and challenging manner, she reminded him of a lioness defending her cub.

As for the baby… Something jerked around Emilio's heart as he studied the boy. The dark Latino coloring was like his own family's, but he could see traces of Cassidy, as well. Dirty face and all, the child was perfection.

So this was Arturo's son.

He found his voice. "Grace Chandler? My name is Emilio Santana."

"I know who you are." Her arms tightened around the baby. "My question is, what are you doing here?"

"This may take some time. May I come in?"

"Of course." Despite the courteous words, she was visibly bristling with distrust as she stepped aside for him to enter. The house was small but tastefully furnished and well kept. Emilio saw no sign of a man about the place, and the woman wasn't wearing a ring. Good—that would make things simpler.

"Please sit down," she said, nodding toward a leather armchair. "When you rang the doorbell, I was about to clean up this baby and change him. If you'll excuse me—"

"Take your time. I can wait."

As she headed down the hall, Emilio settled back in the chair. He was grateful for the chance to compose his thoughts. The impact of seeing his brother's son had staggered him. He was still grappling with his emotions. But one thing was already certain. Young Zac was his last link to Arturo and the heir to the Santana name. The boy was Emilio's insurance that, whether he married or not, the family legacy would continue. He would not be going back to Peru without him.

As for the boy's aunt… He'd managed some online research during his private flight from Lima. Grace Chandler, he'd learned, was an accomplished children's book illustrator. The website he'd found hadn't included a photo, so her chiseled, blonde good looks had come as a pleasant surprise—especially those long, golden legs…

But he would tuck that thought away for a more suitable time.

He surveyed the small room—the colorful cushions, the shelves filled with books, the thriving green plants in hand-made pots and the guitar propped in one corner. Everything looked comfortable and well cared for, though certainly a far cry from the luxury he was accustomed to.

His wandering gaze found a photograph on a low shelf. It showed Cassidy, leaning over an iron railing with the sky behind her. Her emerald eyes were dancing, her rich auburn hair fluttering in the wind. His throat tightened. How could anyone so full of life be gone?

Those weeks that she'd stayed in their home she'd seemed in perfect health. But now Emilio remembered the headaches that had plagued her every few days. Had Cassidy known, even then, that she was dying?

Was it possible that she'd *set out* to get pregnant with Arturo's child?

Emilio burned with questions—and his only hope of answers lay with Grace Chandler.

Grace's hands shook as she taped Zac's diaper in place and fastened the clean blue onesie between his plump little legs. At least now he'd look presentable for…dared she even think the word? His *uncle?*

How could this have happened? After Arturo's letter, she'd believed it was safe to go ahead with the adoption. She'd started making a lifetime of plans for her stepsister's son. Now a dark-eyed stranger who'd appeared out of nowhere could change everything. Had Arturo sent him, or had Emilio Santana come on his own?

More important, what did he want?

Settling Zac in the safety of his crib, she pulled off her soiled shirt and replaced it with a clean, black V-necked top. That done, she yanked off her terry cloth sweatband, splashed her face clean and gave her shoulder-length hair a few licks with the brush—after rinsing away the traces of carrot mush. Even as she tidied up, she knew her appearance didn't matter. She wasn't the one her visitor had come to see. Her instincts told her that Emilio Santana had come for Zac.

And she meant to fight him with everything she had.

He rose as she returned to the living room with Zac in her arms. In faded jeans, an open-necked white shirt and casual black jacket he looked as elegant as a movie hero. It occurred to Grace that she could've taken the baby, crept out the back door and driven away in her car. But she knew it wouldn't have made any difference. A man like Emilio Santana would have the means to track her down anywhere.

"Will he come to me?"

"He's not used to strangers. Sit down. I'll give him a chance to check you out." Grace lowered herself to the ottoman and put Zac on the rug. "Sorry I don't have a drink to offer you, Mr. Santana—unless you'd settle for iced tea. I wasn't expecting company."

"Please call me Emilio. And don't worry about the tea." He took his seat. His English was flawless, his accented voice deep and rich. If she'd closed her eyes, Grace might have pictured Antonio Banderas. But this unsettling man was even better-looking.

Zac had decided to investigate the visitor. He was crawling on all fours toward the chair where Emilio sat. Grace resisted the urge to reach out and pull him back. She'd been present at Zac's birth and first held him when he was only minutes old. She had loved him from the moment Cassidy told her she had a baby on the way. If this presumptuous man thought she was just going to hand over her child and walk away…

"What's his full name?" Emilio was studying the baby. "Izac? Zachary?"

"It's plain Zac—Cassidy's choice. Zac Miller, legally, although I plan to change the last name to my own when the adoption becomes final." Grace emphasized the word *when*.

"I understand you're no blood relation to the boy."

The knot in Grace's stomach tightened. "No, but Cassidy wanted me to raise him. And I have a letter from your brother, consenting to the adoption."

"I know. I've seen a copy of that letter. I found it when I was going through my brother's files." His voice went flat. "Arturo's dead. He was killed in a car crash last month."

Grace felt her heart drop. She stared at Emilio, waiting for the second blow that was sure to come.

"I checked the status of Zac's adoption. I know it hasn't been finalized. As the executor of my brother's estate, I'm asking you to put it on hold."

"Why?" Grace's question emerged as a croak. Her heart was pounding. She felt vaguely nauseous.

"My brother agreed to the adoption on condition that the boy have nothing to do with our family since he planned to marry and start a family with his wife. But his death has changed everything. As far as I know, this boy is Arturo's only child."

Zac had reached the chair and used the padded arm to pull himself to his feet. He stood looking up at Emilio with eyes that would melt granite. Emilio brushed a fingertip across the silky curls—a subtle gesture of possession.

Grace snatched the baby into her arms. "So you want to take him. What if I say no?"

His stony expression answered her challenge. "I've already

contacted my lawyers in Los Angeles. If necessary, they're prepared to block the adoption and bring the matter to court."

Grace's arms tightened around Zac's warm little body. The adoption had already cost her thousands. She had no resources left for a prolonged legal battle. But how could she give up this precious child to be raised by strangers?

"There are stronger ties than blood," she said. "One of them is love. Zac is my son in every way that matters. Nothing could force me to let him go."

"I understand."

"Do you?"

"And do *you,* Grace?" His obsidian eyes drilled into hers. "To my knowledge, my brother sired no other children. This boy could be the heir to more than you've ever dreamed of. You love him like a son—don't you want what's best for him? I have a plan in mind. At least hear me out."

"We don't need your family's money, if that's what you're implying. I earn enough to get by, and Cassidy left a trust fund for Zac's education."

"Listen to me." His voice rasped with impatience. "This isn't about money. It's about the boy. You seem to be the only mother he knows. Separating the two of you would be cruel— and whatever you may think of me, I'm not a cruel man. I cared for Cassidy as a friend and I want her son to be happy."

Grace stared at him in confusion. Now what? Did he intend to leave and let her keep Zac?

"I'm proposing to take the two of you back to Peru with me," he said. "You could see the estate where Zac would grow up and the privileged life he'd enjoy. After that you'd have three choices. You could give him up to my custody and go home, you could work out some kind of visitation arrangement with me, or you could choose to stay in Peru and raise the boy to manhood."

As his words sank home, Grace felt the shock all the way

to her bones. This, then, was her reality. Emilio Santana was Zac's biological uncle. He intended to take his nephew. Her only option was whether or not she would agree to go with him, and leave her life in Arizona behind. If she tried to keep Zac there with her, this man had the power to raise an army of lawyers against her.

She inhaled shakily. "You're saying, if I stayed in Peru, I could take care of Zac, but I couldn't adopt him."

"That's right. It would be your choice."

She rose to face him, holding the baby tight. "But I wouldn't be his mother. I'd be more like his nanny."

Emilio's eyes narrowed. His look was dark and dangerous. "You'd be part of his life. The only other option is to let him go for good."

TWO

Grace pressed close to the window as the Gulfstream G500 dropped toward Lima. Far to the west, the setting sun streaked the clouds with rose and flame. Below the plane, breathtakingly close, the craggy peaks of the Andes jutted into the thin air like ice-tipped daggers.

"Unbelievable," she murmured.

"Isn't it? I never get tired of flying home." Emilio emerged from the cockpit where he'd been consulting with his private pilot. Grace was still getting used to his way of making things happen. Within a few hours of their first meeting, he'd pulled strings to secure the couriered delivery of visas from the Peruvian consulate for her and Zac. Grace had been given just one day to pack and recruit a friend to house-sit. The next morning she and Zac had been picked up and driven to the airport in a chauffeured limousine. Bypassing the hassle of ticket and security lines, they'd been whisked along a side road to Emilio's private plane. Almost before she'd realized it, she was having hot coffee and flaky cheese croissants in the air, served by a slim young man who fussed over Zac and smiled at her efforts to make herself understood in her high school Spanish.

To paraphrase Dorothy in *The Wizard of Oz,* she wasn't in Arizona anymore. She and Zac had been swept up by this cyclone of a man and transported to another world—a world that, for Grace, was still shrouded in unreality.

"How is the boy doing?" Emilio slid into the leather seat across the aisle. He'd spent much of the flight in the office section of the plane, leaving Grace to tend Zac in the main cabin. Maybe he hadn't wanted to impose his presence on her; or, more likely, he simply hadn't had much interest in her company. As his nephew's caretaker, her status wasn't far above a servant's.

Grace glanced toward Zac, who lay strapped in his car seat, sound asleep. "The little pill spent most of the day wearing himself out," she said. "I'm hoping he's down for the count. I know I am."

Emilio's gaze lingered on the sleeping baby, as if examining each feature for traces of his brother. "He's a beautiful child, isn't he?"

"He had a beautiful mother." Grace squelched the urge to remind him what Cassidy had gone through to carry and deliver her baby, refusing needed medicines to treat her cancer that might have caused him harm. All that Arturo had given up was a minuscule blob of DNA—and that while thoroughly enjoying himself. Emilio had contributed nothing at all. The idea that this man was entitled to storm into her life and snatch away the child she loved was unthinkable. But that was her new reality.

"You look tired, Grace." Emilio's gaze took in her drooping hair and tired face. Even after the long day, he looked maddeningly fresh and unrumpled in khakis and a simple polo shirt that matched the black armband he wore as a sign of mourning. Even the faint stubble on his jaw looked as if it was meant to be there.

"In my house you'll have all the help you need," he said. "You'll be able to see the countryside, pursue your art, anything you like—an advantage I suspect you didn't enjoy at home."

Grace hummed noncommittally. Admittedly, the thought of having some help sounded nice. So far, Zac had been a full-time job. But was there more behind Emilio's offer? If Emilio were to marry—as he almost certainly would—his wife would most likely push her aside, forcing her to leave the boy. Was Emilio preparing for that possibility by increasing Zac's dependence on the household servants instead of her?

Emilio glanced out the window. "We're coming into Lima, Grace. Come over here. You'll see more from this side of the plane."

He rose, giving her room to slip into the space next to the window. She felt the hot tingle of awareness as her body brushed his. He was warm and solid through his clothes, his skin smelling lightly of sage-scented soap.

Pulling past him she took her seat. Did he know that her pulse had surged as they touched? But why even speculate? Emilio Santana was well aware of his effect on women— even on *this* woman who had every reason to dislike him. For such a man, seduction would come as naturally as breathing.

But Grace had no intention of falling under his spell. Simple wariness of his wealth and influence had been enough to get her to uproot her life and halt proceedings on the adoption she wanted more than anything. If she actually gave in to his charm, who knew what he could convince her to do?

"Down there." His hands framed her shoulders, turning her toward the view. The mountains had fallen away to a pale ribbon of coastline, surprisingly bleak.

"The mountains keep the rain from reaching the coast." Emilio's hands remained on her shoulders, the contact triggering subtle whorls of heat. "In Lima, the precious little water we get comes mostly from fog and wells. Look, you can see the city lights from here."

The twilight mist was rolling in from the sea, softening the vast river of light that was the capital city of Peru. As the plane glided in on approach, the city unfolded below—a panorama of ancient churches, towering skyscrapers, open plazas and streams of evening traffic. On the outskirts of the city ramshackle slums clung to the barren hillsides.

"Will we be staying in Lima tonight?" Grace asked.

"We'll just be touching down to refuel, check you and the boy through immigration, and load some supplies. Then we'll be flying on to Cusco. My driver will be waiting there with the car. It's a spectacular flight. You won't be seeing much tonight, but there'll be plenty of other chances.

"So we'll have to deplane for immigration?" Grace glanced over at the sleeping Zac, a sigh escaping her lips as she imagined standing in a long line with a cranky baby in her arms.

"Don't worry about it. I'll just show your papers to the right people. They know me. If there's any question, they can board the plane and meet you in person."

So easy. No doubt some cash would be changing hands. Grace had heard it was the accepted way of getting things done in this part of the world. She had never approved of what she viewed as bribery. But tonight she was too tired to stand on principle.

Minutes later the landing gear dropped and the wheels touched down. The tanker truck was waiting on the tarmac. By the time the refueling was finished, Emilio had taken care of the paperwork and returned to the plane. "All done."

He handed Grace her stamped passport. "I told you there would be no problem."

"I must say I'm impressed," she countered. "But whatever you did to speed things along, I don't want to know about it."

"You *Norteamericanos!* So proper!" He chuckled, his grin a white flash in the darkness of the cabin. "Look at it this way, Grace. You are happy because you didn't have to wake the baby and wait in line for your papers. My friend in *Migración* is happy because he can now pay his rent. Our pilot is happy because he'll be home in time for dinner. And I am happy because everyone else is happy. What do you see here that is not good?"

Grace's only answer was a weary sigh as she buckled her seat belt for the takeoff. "How long will we be in the car once we land?" she asked, changing the subject.

"Not long. It's an hour's drive from Cusco to Urubamba. You can sleep on the way if you get tired. There'll be blankets and pillows in the backseat, and some fresh baby formula in case the boy wakes up hungry."

"His name is Zac."

There was a beat of awkward silence. "But of course," Emilio said.

As the plane rose skyward again, Grace studied his profile against the window. For a powerful, confident man, he seemed ill at ease with his newly discovered nephew. She suspected he'd never spent time with children before. If the jet-setting, thrill-seeking lifestyle she'd seen highlighted in the tabloids was accurate then she doubted he'd ever taken responsibility for another person in his life.

If that was true, she already had her work cut out for her. It wouldn't be easy, helping a man change the habits from a lifetime of no consequences and disposable relationships, but this was *one* relationship Grace intended to see Emilio take seriously. If he was going to claim custody of Cassidy's precious son, she would make sure *the Peruvian Playboy* learned to be a father to Zac. Not just a father, but a *dad*.

The silver-gray Audi purred along the mountain road, gearing down on the hairpin curves. The narrow highway from Cusco to Urubamba could be dangerous after dark, and Emilio had warned his driver to take extra care. Tonight there was precious cargo on board.

On the far side of the backseat, Grace had fallen asleep, her tousled blonde head pillowed in the corner between the seat and the window. Feeling an unaccustomed tenderness, Emilio had tucked a blanket around her as she slept. She'd had her whole life uprooted, but she'd kept her complaints to herself. All she'd asked of him was to let her be with the child she loved—a child who wasn't even hers. He couldn't help but admire that kind of devotion. For all her stubborn independence, Grace Chandler was a genuinely good woman. Arturo's son was lucky to have her.

The baby slumbered between them, securely buckled into his car seat. In the semidarkness, Emilio studied the chubby features—the pert nose and dimpled chin, the straight brows and feathery black eyelashes. He saw more of Cassidy than his brother in the child. But that would change. Like all Santana males, young Zac would grow to be a tall, handsome man. By the time he came of age, he would already be learning to run the estate and the Santana business empire.

Such big responsibilities for a little boy. Little Zac should have his father here to teach him. *Tio* Emilio would have to fill the void. Heart skipping, Emilio brushed a fingertip across the soft ridge of knuckles. Zac stirred and whimpered, causing Emilio to pull away. Had he done something wrong? *Por diós,* he didn't know the first thing about babies.

With Arturo gone, duty demanded that he be a father to this *niño precioso*. But how could he even begin?

Emilio remembered his own father as a busy, distant man who'd suffered a fatal heart attack at fifty, leaving a mistress in Callao and a twenty-year-old son as the head of the family. Arturo had been yanked out of Harvard and forced to grow up fast. Emilio, barely seventeen, had been left to drift.

Their mother, a pampered society beauty, had been little help. She'd taken to her bed for the first few months, then flung herself into a series of sad affairs that ended one night in a fatal mix of pills and alcohol.

In short, Emilio had barely ever known what it was like even to have a parent—he'd certainly never learned to *be* a parent. To him, this small lump of humanity was more intimidating than a boardroom full of corporate rivals bent on eating him alive.

"A penny for your thoughts." Grace's husky voice startled him. She'd awakened and was studying him with her extraordinary hazel eyes. Tangled hair framed her sleepy face. She looked surprisingly sexy, he thought. He was struck by the intimate feel of the moment—the dark, close atmosphere of the car's backseat; her presence beside him, warm, drowsy and more relaxed than he'd ever seen her, speaking to him in a soft, languorous voice.

"I asked you what you were thinking." She spoke as if explaining her previous question. Knowing she might not be pleased by the truth, Emilio scrambled for a diversion.

"Tell me about Cassidy," he said.

"Didn't you know her when she was here?"

"We had a few conversations. But she didn't mention her family or her illness."

"There wasn't much family to tell you about. We were teenagers when her father married my mother. At first we had nothing in common. She was the beautiful, wild one. I was the older, serious one. We alternated between fighting and ignoring each other. But after our parents died in a plane crash we became close. I took care of her until she was old enough to leave home and get modeling work. Wherever she went, we kept in touch."

"What about the brain tumor?" he asked. "Cassidy had headaches in Peru, but she never mentioned…" He shook his head. "I keep wondering if she knew, even then."

"Cassidy had surgery and radiation for the tumor six years ago, when she was twenty-two. The doctors said it might come back. When she started having headaches again, yes, she knew what it was."

"And the baby?"

"Soon after she got home, she discovered she was pregnant. The doctors advised an abortion. Cassidy wouldn't hear of it. She even made us promise that if we had to, we'd keep her body on life support long enough to safely deliver the baby. But that turned out not to be necessary. She lived to hold her son and name him…and to give him to me." Grace gulped back a surge of tears. "She sacrificed so much to bring him into the world."

Emilio pondered what she'd told him. "She's not the only one. It's a big sacrifice you've made, too, uprooting your life to bring him here, to a strange country—"

Her eyes flashed in the darkness. "Zac *is* my life. There's nothing I've left behind that matters as much to me as him."

"But your house, your work—"

"My house will be there. And once my art supplies are unpacked, I can work almost anywhere. All I need is a little space."

"If you wish to work, of course, there'll be room for you to set up a studio." Emilio said. "Not that you'll need the income. If you decide to stay, you'll receive pay and lodging for being in charge of my brother's son."

Her body went rigid, jerking her bolt upright in the seat. Emilio knew at once he'd said the wrong thing. But he didn't know how make it right.

He spoke against the icy wall of her silence. "You'll also have a car and driver at your disposal. A pretty woman driving alone in this country is asking for trouble."

Of course he would see to it that she had everything she required while she was here and taking care of the boy. It was only fair. No matter what she said, he knew she'd given up a great deal. Room and board, plus an income for whatever else she needed, were little enough for him to provide.

Her full lower lip quivered. "Is that all you think I am to Zac? Just his hired caretaker?"

So that was what he'd said wrong. Emilio exhaled, easing the frustration that had surged like heat in a volcano. "Of course not. I'm just trying to do the right thing—for you, for Zac and for my family's future."

She was silent for a moment, studying him with those arresting eyes. They still danced with anger, but she seemed to be holding it in. "Tell me about your family," she said, surprising him.

"As you said about your own family, there's not much to tell. I lost my parents fifteen years ago. My firstborn brother died when he was four. Then there was Arturo…and me. That's all."

"What about Arturo's wife? He told me he was getting married."

"The wedding never happened. Arturo kept finding excuses to put it off. He said he was busy with work. But I think the truth was he never got over Cassidy."

Her gaze deepened in the shadows. "So you're the last of the Santanas."

Emilio glanced at the sleeping baby. "Not anymore."

By the time the car reached the outskirts of Urubamba, Zac was awake and fussing. Grace found the formula stored in the portable cooler. Soon he was chugging it down, clasping the bottle like a pro. Before long he'd be old enough to

wean to a sippy cup, and after that there'd be walking, talking, potty training—so many ways a little boy would need
a mother's help. How could she ever think of going back to
Arizona and leaving him to the care of hired nursemaids?

Emilio sniffed and frowned. "I think somebody might
need changing."

Grace nodded, recognizing the familiar stink. "That's no
surprise. But I was hoping I wouldn't have to change him
in the car."

"I was hoping the same thing. If it can wait a few more
minutes, we'll be home."

Home to a place she'd never been before. The line from
the old John Denver song flickered through Grace's mind.
But even without seeing much of it, she knew this strange
country would never be home to her. It could be Zac's home,
though. And if this was what was best for Zac, then she'd
find a way to deal with it. For now, she'd have to try to look
on the bright side of things.

And that would include finding humor where she could…
such as in the way Emilio was edging away from Zac, toward his side of the car. "Have you ever changed a baby?"
she asked, amused at his discomfort.

"No, and I don't plan to."

"Why? I've known some very manly men who don't mind
changing a diaper."

"In your country, maybe. Not in mine. I would not even
know where to begin."

"Well, in that case, maybe I should give you a demonstra-
tion." Opening the diaper bag, she made a show of fumbling
for the things she'd need.

His hand flashed out and caught her wrist. "Please not
now, and not in this car!"

As she met his concerned gaze, Grace couldn't help it. She
had to giggle. A dimple deepened in her cheek.

Muttering a curse in Spanish, he released her and sank back against the seat. "So you're teasing me! You're a vixen, Grace Chandler!"

"I've been called worse." Grace closed the diaper bag. "I'll give you a break this time. But take warning, Emilio, if you're going to raise a baby, you'll have to get used to everything that comes with being a father!"

A startled expression flickered across his face. Was it because she'd had the effrontery to stand up to him, or had he just realized that he'd be responsible for acting as a father for his brother's son? Taking on a child as heir was one thing, but becoming a parent was another matter entirely. Was he up to the challenge?

The question fled her mind as the car swung off the highway and onto a graveled road that crunched beneath the wheels. Leafy branches overhung the long, narrow drive, forming a filigreed canopy that let in shafts of silver moonlight.

The lights of a small gatehouse shone through the darkness. A uniformed guard stepped out to open the wrought-iron gate. Grace shivered as she glimpsed the holstered pistol at his hip.

"We're home, Grace," Emilio said.

Home—a place she'd never been before.

Three

Grace opened her eyes. Blinding sunlight streamed through the open shutters of a grilled window. Dazed, she rolled away from the glare. What time was it?

The hands on the bedside clock pointed to 9:15. She groaned, remembering that most of South America was east of the United States. Peru would be on New York time. But her jet-lagged brain was still waking up in Arizona.

Zac must be on Arizona time, too. She had yet to hear a peep from the old-fashioned crib in the corner of the spacious bedroom.

Sinking back into the pillow she closed her eyes and allowed herself the luxury of a slow wake-up. They'd arrived last night in darkness, the house a sprawling hacienda behind high stone walls. After Emilio vanished, a stocky woman in local dress had shown Grace to this bedroom, with its adjoining marble bath. After a few moments of fussing over Zac, the woman had left her alone to put the baby to bed and brush her teeth. Too tired to unpack her pajamas, she'd stripped down to her underwear and crawled between lavender-scented sheets. The next thing Grace remembered it was morning.

Opening her eyes again, she scanned her surroundings. The massive four-poster bed looked as if it had been hand-hewn centuries ago from one giant tree. The canopy was draped in white netting, as was Zac's crib in the far corner of the room. The downy coverlet was finished in a wine-colored brocade that contrasted richly with the open-timbered ceiling and whitewashed walls.

Like the bed frame, the dresser was lavishly carved, with a full-length mirror and matching velvet-topped bench. There were no closets, but a row of elegant wooden wardrobes stood along one wall. Clearly, this was no ordinary guest room. It had been built and furnished for someone with clothes to fill the wardrobes and adornments to justify the tall, gilt-framed mirror above the dresser. Grace tried to imagine generations of Santana men and women. How many of them had lived, loved and died in this room—and in this bed?

Grace hadn't even known her own grandparents. How would it feel to have a family history going back for generations?

Roused to wakefulness, she swung her feet to the tiles and pattered over to the crib to check on Zac, who had yet to make a sound.

Grace parted the layered netting. Staring down into the crib, she gasped.

Zac was gone.

Tearing into her suitcase, she found her black nylon travel robe, flung it on and yanked the ties into a knot. Her motherly instincts were screaming. Her baby was missing in a strange place. What if he'd climbed or fallen out of bed and crawled away in the night? She had to find him.

Still barefoot, she burst out of the door and into a shadowed hallway. Grace froze, ears straining in the silence. She'd had nightmares like this—racing through dark passageways, searching for Zac. But this nightmare was real.

A faint light, barely visible, suggested a corner at the hall's far end. She raced toward it, only to find herself looking down another long passageway. The house seemed as confusing as a giant labyrinth. But she would find Zac if she had to search every square foot of it.

Rounding the next corner at full tilt, she slammed into something big and solid. She staggered backward. Powerful hands caught her, steadying her shoulders.

"Grace?" Emilio's dark eyes gazed down at her. "What's wrong?"

"Zac's gone. He's not in his crib!"

For the space of a breath he seemed to be studying her, taking stock of her tousled hair, her tired eyes and the short, black travel robe. Glancing down as well, she noticed that the robe had slipped off one shoulder, revealing her bra strap and the curve of her breast. Self-conscious, she tugged it back into place.

His troubled expression eased. His mouth twitched, as if biting back a chuckle. "Zac is fine, Grace. He woke up early, so the maids took him to the kitchen. He's having a grand time in there."

Grace felt herself crumbling. Relief washed through her at the knowledge that Zac was safe, but the feeling was quickly replaced with a rush of shame. She'd slept through Zac waking up? That had never happened before. Yes, she'd been exhausted after the flight, but that was no excuse. What must Emilio think of her, to be failing at her responsibilities to care for Zac on their very first day in Peru?

"What's this? Tears?" Emilio thumbed her chin, tilting her face upward. He was freshly shaved and showered, his black hair glistening with moisture. Dressed in jeans, boots and a gray T-shirt that displayed his broad chest and muscular shoulders, he looked so annoyingly handsome that she could have punched the look off his face that seemed so mockingly sympathetic.

"Don't make fun of me, Emilio," she muttered. "Look at me. I'm still shaking. I was scared to death."

His fingertips skimmed along her jaw, brushing her earlobe as he released her. Grace willed herself to ignore the heat that flashed through her like desert lightning.

"Poor Grace." His voice was a velvet caress. "I understand your being frightened. What mother wouldn't be?"

His words doused her arousal immediately, leaving her cold and aching. No doubt, they were innocently meant. Emilio could have no way of knowing that she could never truly be a mother. Zac had been her one best chance—a chance that might never come again.

"Can I take you to the kitchen?" Emilio offered. "You can see for yourself that Zac is fine."

Torn between urgency and embarrassment, Grace glanced down at her bare feet and the thin robe that barely covered her thighs. "I can't go like this."

"Certainly you can!" Emilio captured her hand. "This is my home and you're my guest. The staff's used to people parading around here in all sorts of dress—or lack of dress, if you will."

"I can just imagine," Grace muttered as he led her along the corridor. If Zac was to grow up here, some aspects of Emilio's playboy lifestyle would have to change.

The passage opened up to a covered portico with feathery palms in exquisite ceramic pots. Beyond the pillars Grace glimpsed a patio with a fountain that looked as if it could have been tinkling away for centuries. As Arturo's heir, this magnificent estate would be part of Zac's legacy. The boy would have the best of everything, including the finest education money could buy. And what could she offer him as a single mother? A modest house. A public school education…

Wafting aromas of bacon and coffee told her they were nearing the kitchen. Now she could hear voices—women's voices, laughing and chattering.

"This way." Emilio guided her around an elbow bend in the passageway, designed to conceal the kitchen entry. A few more steps, and Grace found herself in a sunny, spacious kitchen, furnished with modern appliances and decorated in colorful tiles. Gleaming copper pans hung above the massive stove. Strings of dried peppers, onions, garlic and vanilla pods trailed along the wall above an ancient stone fireplace.

In the far corner, next to a window, Zac perched in a well-scrubbed wooden high chair. Two young maids in native dress were hand-feeding him slices of ripe banana, giggling as he mashed the food in his fingers and stuffed it in his mouth. Zac was hooting with delight, enjoying the attention.

Turning, he caught sight of Grace. For an instant he looked surprised. Then his dark puppy eyes lit. He grinned, waved his sticky hands and spoke his very first word.

"Mama!"

Grace's heart dropped and shattered.

Emilio watched Grace rush across the kitchen. He'd caught the glint of tears as she broke away. Many women had used tears to manipulate him, and he thought he'd become hardened to the sight. But Grace's tears, welling in those magnificent hazel eyes that were overflowing with deep, maternal love, had moved him in an unexpected way.

His own mother had left him to be raised by servants while she pursued her life of socializing, shopping and beauty treatments. She'd given him little attention, let alone affection. Now, seeing a woman shed tears of love for a child who wasn't even biologically hers came as a shock.

For the first time, Emilio questioned the benevolence of taking Arturo's son. How could he tear a child from the arms of the only mother he'd ever known—a mother who clearly loved him?

Only one solution would ease his guilt—persuading Grace to stay and raise the boy here. She'd agreed to come to Peru— that was a big step. But he knew the battle wasn't over when it came to convincing her to stay. She was a foreigner who would be giving up a good life in the United States. Some aspects of his culture would be unfamiliar, even disturbing. But if she decided to leave, one thing was certain—Zac would not be going with her. The boy belonged here.

Grace had reached the high chair and was bending over to wash Zac's face. Her pose gave him a tantalizing glimpse of leopard-print panties and a shapely rump, with those long, golden legs stretching below. Emilio swore under his breath. Seducing Grace would be delicious. It might even induce her to be content to stay around. But what would happen when the magic faded, as it always did? It would be the same old story—accusations, tears, slamming doors and a hasty drive to the airport.

Emilio knew the routine well. Most of the time he didn't mind. The end of one affair opened the door for another. But Grace's departure would only create problems—not the least of them, a miserable child. Even if she stayed after the breakup, the awkwardness would make things unpleasant, especially if he brought in new *compañeras*.

With a sigh of regret, Emilio faced the truth. If he wanted to keep Grace here, he'd be a fool to lay so much as a lustful finger on the woman. He would need to treat her like a sister.

She'd straightened now, but the view of her body in that silky little robe was enough to tighten his briefs. Emilio mut-

tered an appreciative curse. If this kept up, he'd be spending
time under a cold shower.

Looking for a diversion he glanced at his watch. "Grace."
She turned, her sun-streaked hair tumbling over one eye.
Emilio cleared the tightness from his throat. "If you can be
ready in half an hour, I'll meet you on the patio for breakfast. Then I'll show you around. All right?"

"Sure." She turned her attention back to the baby and the
two maids. Feeling as if he'd been dismissed, Emilio returned
to the portico and crossed the open patio to the ancient library
that served as his home office. It was a magnificent room, the
walls lined with shelves of priceless books, the rich leather
couches arranged for socializing or reading. The computer
on the ancient desk looked out of place with its ugly cords
and connections. For now, at least, that couldn't be helped.

Taking his seat, Emilio turned on the power and brought
up his email. After deleting the messages he judged not to
be worth reading, he opened one from a longtime friend, the
Greek shipping heir Nikolas Stavros.

Sorry to hear about your brother, Emilio. You'll have plenty
to deal with, but hoping you'll be free for my April party
cruise. Won't drop names here but some old friends will be
on board, as well as a certain hot TV actress who says she's
dying to meet you. Your usual cabin's reserved and waiting.
Nik

With a weary breath, Emilio typed his regrets and pressed
Send. Before Arturo's accident he'd have looked forward to a
wild week of sex and partying on his friend's palatial yacht.
But those days were over. By the time he saw his way clear
of running the Santana fiefdom, he'd be an old man.

And for what? His parents were long gone. Even while

they were alive, they'd had no time for him. What did he owe them?

To hell with it. He could sell off everything but the estate and live in freedom for the rest of his life. Why not just do it?

Emilio ran a restless hand through his unruly curls. Arturo, four years his senior, had been mostly gray by the time he died. Emilio was beginning to understand how that could happen.

Emilio had never expected to take Arturo's place—never wanted to. The burden had dropped on him with the crushing weight of an avalanche. And up until a week ago, he'd thought that as the last surviving Santana male, he was destined to bear that weight alone.

But now, everything had changed. Now, there was Zac. His brother's little boy. The heir to everything the family had built over countless generations. And now that he had someone to work for, someone to pass the legacy on to, Emilio started to understand the drive to protect the investments and secure the future so that the next generation would inherit something of value.

He owed it to Zac, who needed him, and to Arturo, who had never given up on him, to do his best for the family. *His* family.

A family that now included a member who was far too alluring. He found her an intriguing woman—intelligent, challenging and sensual. The fact that he'd declared her off-limits made her all the more tantalizing; but he'd resolved not to think of her in those terms. He was capable of being friends with an attractive woman. He'd proven that with Cassidy. He could do the same with Grace if it was in his family's best interests.

Meanwhile he needed to go over the accounts for the estate, familiarizing himself with the monthly salaries and expenses, and making sure everything was paid to date. He'd already learned that the old hacienda didn't support itself, but depended on the income from other ventures. The Santana empire was an interconnected web, so complicated that the thought of it made Emilio's head ache. But the mess was his responsibility now, and he knew better than to think he could walk away from it.

With a glance at his watch, he set to work.

The day was already warm when Grace returned to her room to get ready for breakfast. After a quick shower, Grace dressed in khaki shorts, a plain white shirt, leather sandals and, as an afterthought, gold gypsy earrings. She'd expected to be bathing Zac, but the maids, Ana and Eugenia, had commandeered the boy. As nearly as Grace could make out with her limited Spanish, the two girls were sisters with four younger siblings at home. They seemed very competent with Zac, who was smiling and jabbering, basking in their attention. Surrendering to their pleas, Grace had given them Zac's clean clothes and diapers and gone to get ready herself.

The older woman Grace had met last night caught up with her in the hallway and guided her back to the patio off the dining area. *"Aquí está, señorita,"* she murmured, indicating a sunny table with two chairs. *"Don Emilio llegará en un momento."*

Grace congratulated herself on having understood that Emilio would be here in a moment. She took her seat with a polite *"Gracias."*

The woman poured rich black coffee. *"El niño es hijo de Don Arturo?"* she asked.

Again Grace understood. The woman was asking whether Zac was Arturo's son. *"Sí,"* she responded, fumbling for the words. *"Es hijo de Arturo y de mi hermana."* Had she said it correctly, that Zac was the son of Arturo and her sister? The woman's smile told her she'd succeeded.

The woman pointed to her chest. *"Me llamo* Dolores."

"Mucho gusto, Dolores. *Me llamo* Grace." The old high school Spanish was coming back.

"A su servicio, señorita." With a nod of her graying head, Dolores hurried away. Settling back in her chair Grace sipped her coffee and took in the view. This patio was larger than the one she'd crossed earlier. Bougainvillea, riotous with pink blooms, cascaded from the eaves. A spacious wrought-iron cage held two scarlet macaws. They fluttered and squabbled, feasting on scraps of fruit.

A cobbled path meandered through a grove of flowering trees. Not far beyond, Grace glimpsed a swimming pool. A shirtless young man with a taut, muscular body was skimming the water with a long-handled net. In the distance, steep mountains, bare of trees, towered against the sky.

"Here you are." Emilio strode onto the patio. "Sorry if I'm late. Just catching up on some work."

"No problem. I've been enjoying the view. I didn't expect to have so much time on my hands, but it seems Ana and Eugenia have taken over—" Grace almost said *my son,* but she caught herself. "They've taken over the baby. They even insisted on bathing him."

"That doesn't surprise me. But you don't need to worry. They're good girls and very capable." Emilio slid into his chair, his eyes taking her measure from her gypsy hoops to her low-heeled leather sandals. "You look…nice." He paused before the last word as if he'd been about to say something else.

"Thanks. This is about as dressed-up as you'll see me while I'm here."

"Oh?" Emilio poured his coffee and took a sip. "That's too bad because I'm planning a party next weekend to welcome you and my brother's son to Peru. I was looking forward to seeing you in an evening dress."

"Oh, but I didn't bring—"

"Of course you wouldn't have packed a gown. But there are fine shops in Cusco. My driver can take you after you're settled in."

Dolores had come outside with a tray of beautifully cut tropical fruits—pineapple, mango, melon and banana. "It's almost too pretty to eat!" Grace speared several pieces for her plate.

"Get used to it. When it comes to food, Dolores is a true artist. The two girls you met are her nieces. She's training them to take her place one day—as her father trained her in this very kitchen."

The food kept coming—airy scrambled eggs, crisp slabs of bacon, seasoned black beans, fried potatoes and buttered corn muffins. Everything was so delicious that Grace had to push herself away from the table. "Heavens, do you eat like this every day?" she asked.

Emilio had been watching her devour breakfast, a knowing twinkle in his eyes. "Again, you'll get accustomed to it. In the city, meals are more like what you're used to. But here in Urubamba we follow tradition—a hearty breakfast to start the day, a light lunch around two o'clock followed by a siesta—when there's time for it, at least. Then at night, around nine o'clock, we dress up and gather for dinner. It's all very civilized."

He finished his plate and put his napkin on the table. "If you're finished I'd like to show you the countryside. By chance, do you ride?"

Ride? Grace's stomach clenched with instinctive fear. She forced her mouth into a smile. "I rode as a teenager. But I haven't been on a horse in fifteen years. I'm not sure if I even remember how. If you don't mind, I'll walk."

"Nonsense!" he exclaimed, his insistence tightening the knot in her stomach. "We'll have a lot of ground to cover—

too much to travel on foot—and nobody forgets how to ride. I'll find you the gentlest horse in the stable." He glanced down at her bare legs. "You'll want to put on long pants."

Grace rose. It would be simpler to tell him the truth. But the truth was too private, too personal to share. The only other choice was facing stark, paralyzing panic.

"See you back here in fifteen minutes," he said. "I'll find you a hat, and I'll check on the boy for you."

His name is Zac, she wanted to remind him. But her fear-constricted throat refused to form the words.

Four

In the bedroom, Grace shed her shorts and found her blue jeans. Her legs quivered as she stood on the rug to pull them on. Maybe she could tell Emilio she was ill, or make some excuse about Zac needing her. Anything to save her from mounting a horse again.

As she tugged the jeans over her hips, her fingers skimmed the puckered scar that slashed across her belly at the bikini line. Grace had tried to block the old accident from her memory, but the ugly scar would always be there to remind her.

Now the nightmare flashed again—the crunch of hard gravel against her back, the screaming horse, the plummeting hooves and the awful crushing sensation between her hip bones…

Pressing her lips together, she willed the memory to fade. Still it lingered, as sickening as if it had happened yesterday. What she wouldn't give to make it go away?

Maybe Emilio had offered her an answer. For the past

fifteen years, she'd avoided anything to do with horses and riding. Was it time she faced her fear?

Her hands shook as she refastened her sandals, wishing she'd packed something sturdier for her feet. No, she couldn't do it. She would tell Emilio the truth—or at least as much as she felt comfortable sharing. Once he knew, he would never invite her to ride again.

Tucking in her shirt and strapping on her belt, she closed her room and found her way back to the patio. Emilio was waiting for her with a canvas vest over his shirt. "Let's go!" he said, grinning as he plopped a straw hat on her head. "You're going to enjoy this."

She hung back. "Emilio, I can't—"

"Come on!" He caught her hand, pulling her alongside him. "Don't worry, you'll be fine!"

Skirting the pool, they moved across a patch of open lawn. Beyond the trees Grace could see a long, low building that framed one side of a fenced paddock—unmistakably a stable. Her pulse ripped into a frenzied cadence.

"Emilio, stop!" She yanked his arm, jerking him to a halt. Brows furrowed in confusion, he glanced back over his shoulder.

"Listen to me," she said. "Fifteen years ago I had an accident with a horse. I won't go into the details but I was hurt—badly. I haven't ridden since."

Understanding lit his features, and Grace let out a sigh of relief. He'd let this go now.

"Did you ride often before the accident?" he asked.

"Yes, I used to ride all the time."

"Then it's high time you did so again." He turned to face her fully, his eyes riveting her in place. "If you give up something you loved because it hurt you once, you'll regret it for the rest of your life."

He extended his hand, inviting her to take it. Grace

hung back, hesitating. "You don't understand. I'm afraid of horses—terrified if you want to know the truth."

"Do you like being terrified, Grace?"

His question stunned her. She shook her head. "Of course not. I hate it. But how can I change the way I feel?"

A smile teased the corner of his sensual mouth. His hand captured hers and held it gently but firmly. "Come," he said. "Come and meet my beautiful horses."

He led her through the trees to the paddock fence. Beyond the rails, three dark-coated mares grazed while their foals frolicked in the sunlight. They raised their heads at the humans' approach—elegant, compact creatures with tapered muzzles, silky manes and tails that hung straight down between their ample haunches.

As a horse-loving girl, she'd learned to recognize common breeds. These animals, she realized, were all of a kind. But she'd never seen anything like them.

Emilio gave a low whistle. The mares pricked their ears and moved toward him—not trotting but flowing, with a level gait that alternated left and right sides.

"They're Peruvian Pasos," Emilio said, "bred for long days in the saddle. Arturo handled the family business, but these babies are mine."

The mares were nearing the fence. Grace felt the icy band of fear constricting her chest. She tried to back away, but Emilio's hand, pressing the small of her back, stopped her.

"Don't be afraid," he murmured. "They're as gentle as kittens."

The mares crowded the fence, their long-lashed eyes like liquid amber. Their noses butted Emilio's vest, nuzzling at the pockets. He laughed, the sound of a man in his element. "One at a time, ladies. I know you all love me. Here you are—"

He pulled three carrots out of his pockets and fed two of the mares. The third mare nickered impatiently as Emilio handed the last carrot to Grace. "Go ahead. She won't bite you."

Feeding a horse was nothing like riding one, Grace told herself. But her hand shook as she held out the carrot. The mare took it with whoosh of warm breath and the brush of a velvety muzzle. Grace stepped back, limp-kneed with relief.

"Was that so bad?" Emilio asked.

Grace's heart was pounding. Her fear was irrational, but she couldn't help her gut reaction. "I don't think I can do this."

"Then don't think. Just do it. Our horses are saddled and waiting." His insistent hand propelled her toward the stables. "When the morning's over, you'll thank me."

Grace allowed him to guide her. Emilio had flung down a challenge. If she gave in to her fear he would lose a hefty measure of respect for her—respect she was going to need in the days ahead.

Somehow she would have to conquer her terror.

As they came into the stable yard Grace saw two saddled horses. Both were Peruvian Pasos, the smaller one a silver-gray gelding, the larger a stallion, a magnificent golden palomino.

"Those foals in the paddock are his sons," Emilio said. "He sires fine babies, but not yet one of his color."

"A stud? And you ride him?" Grace willed herself not to flinch as the palomino snorted and tossed his handsome head.

"Pasos are the gentlest of horses, even the stallions," Emilio said. "You'll see."

"Me?" Grace swallowed a gasp. "You're going to put me on that horse?"

"Don't worry." Emilio patted the gelding. "You'll be on Manso, here. He's a calm old fellow. A child could ride him."

Manso. Grace took comfort in the name, which meant tame, or gentle. Maybe she'd be all right. Still, her stomach

spasmed as Emilio held the bridle and stepped aside for her
to mount. A cold bead of sweat trickled down her forehead.

She had to do this.

Holding her breath, she placed a sandal in the stirrup and
pushed upward. The horse shuddered as she settled into the
saddle. Grace's pulse surged. "Easy, boy." She stroked the
sleek neck, feeling the warmth of skin beneath her hand. It
was just a leisurely ride, she told herself. She was foolish to
be frightened.

Handing her the reins, Emilio swung onto the stallion.
"Vámonos," he said, taking the lead. "Let's go."

Grace nudged the gelding forward, feeling the unaccustomed flow of the Paso's gait beneath her. The easy sway was
like rocking in a comfortable chair. As they trailed through
the dappled shade her fears began to ease.

The narrow path wound up a rocky hillside. Emilio rode
ahead of her, sitting his horse with the air of a conquistador,
back straight, broad shoulders tapering to narrow hips and
taut buttocks. Tendrils of ebony hair curled low on the back
of his suntanned neck. Grace could almost imagine stroking
them with her fingers as he…

With a mental slap, she jerked herself back to reality.
Emilio was a man who bedded models and movie starlets.
Even if she wanted him—which she told herself she most
certainly did not—she wasn't the sort of woman he'd choose.
She was useful to him; that was all. Having her here to care
for his brother's son was a convenience. She went along with
it because raising the boy here was better than having him
taken from her entirely.

But that didn't mean she'd allow herself to be used. She
would fight for the right to keep Zac close and raise him as
she saw fit. The last thing she wanted was for Cassidy's precious son to become a playboy like Emilio.

The trail widened into an overlook. Emilio reined the palomino and waited for Grace to catch up. Sitting silently, he gave her time to take in the view of the long, green valley, cut through by a tumbling river. Villages and farms dotted the riverbanks. Cattle, donkeys and sheep grazed on stone terraces cut like giant staircases into the hillsides.

"Amazing," she whispered.

"You're looking at the Sacred Valley of the Incas," Emilio said. "The terraces were where they planted their crops."

Gazing farther down the valley, Grace could see more terraced slopes. "So many, and those terraces are huge," she said. "How could people build something like that, with no machines?"

"No one knows. But the Incas were master engineers and builders. You'll see more of their work in Cusco. And one of these days I'll take you to Machu Picchu."

"I've seen photos. The real thing must be breathtaking." Grace lifted her hat and let the breeze cool her damp face. The gelding swished a fly with his tail. Her nerves jumped at the sudden movement, but she held her fear in check. It bolstered her courage, knowing she'd managed to ride this docile horse. Given time, she might even conquer her nightmares.

But where would her life be by then?

"I want you to stay, Grace." Emilio's voice was like warm honey, flowing and persuasive. "You could have a beautiful life here, working on your art and watching Zac grow up. What could be better?"

Having someone to love and a family of my own. That would be better. Grace's reply remained unspoken. There was no point in sharing a dream that she knew would never come true. And anyway, the man didn't care about her happiness. She was a handy solution to the challenge of raising his brother's son while he pursued his women and his carefree life. He wanted her to stay, because it would take the responsibility off his shoulders. Grace was used to having to shoulder responsibility. She'd done it for Cassidy time and time again. But this time, taking on the responsibility would mean giving up her independence. Could she handle that?

"What are you thinking?" His sensual gaze made her tingle with awareness. But this was just part of his game, Grace reminded herself. Seduction would be second nature to a man like Emilio Santana. But it wasn't going to work with her.

She shot him a chilling look. "I'm thinking that it's too soon for a decision. It's a given that I won't be separated from Zac. But I need time to weigh my options. I'm hoping you'll give me that time." In truth, she'd already ruled out every option except staying. But Emilio didn't need to know that. The idea that she might settle for a part-time arrangement or even try to get Zac back was the only bargaining chip she had.

"Take all the time you need." He led the way as they meandered down the slope toward a village. Now and then he paused, pointing out a bird, a flowering tree, a carved stone jutting from the earth. He'd slipped into tour guide mode, pleasant but impersonal.

The village was small, little more than a cluster of adobe dwellings joined by a cobbled street. But it was a busy place. Through an open gate, Grace glimpsed women weaving in a courtyard. Children in spotless school uniforms hurried toward a bus stop. A wandering donkey nibbled at blades of grass between the stones.

"Everywhere I look I see something I want to paint," Grace mused aloud.

"And you've barely begun to see it all." Emilio slowed his horse to let a flock of geese waddle across the road in front of them. "An artist like you would never run out of inspiration here." That much was true, Grace conceded.

Two men in native garb strolled toward an open doorway where a scrap of red cloth fluttered from a pole.

"The red flag on a house means the women have brewed

a fresh batch of *chicha*," Emilio explained. "They're selling it by the glass."

"Sort of like the lemonade stand I had as a kid. I could use a cold drink. Is it any good?"

He chuckled. "It's made from fermented maize. I won't go into what's involved, but trust me, it's an acquired taste."

"Oh." Grace raked back her hair and replaced her hat.

"If you're thirsty, we can get something at one of the tourist hotels in town. Or if you've had enough riding, we could turn around and go home. It's up to you."

"I really should get back to Zac. He's not used to being away from me."

"That's fine. I've got a mountain of paperwork waiting, so I need to get back, too. Dolores keeps cold sodas in the fridge. I'll see that you get one."

He turned the palomino toward the trail. Grace followed on Manso. Riding the placid horse had been a good experience, but enough was enough. She'd be relieved to get her feet on solid ground again.

Still, she couldn't shake the feeling that because she hadn't immediately given in to his request for an answer, she'd been dismissed. It seemed his interest in spending time with her waned when she proved less tractable than he'd expected. Not that she cared, Grace reminded herself. Emilio had more urgent things to do than spend time with her. He was only being a polite host.

They'd crested the trail and were headed downhill through the trees when she heard playful shouts and the sound of boyish laughter. "Just some kids from the village," Emilio said. "See, there they are."

Grace caught sight of two ragged half-grown boys through the trees. Armed with slingshots, they appeared to be shooting at birds. But as soon as they spotted the two riders, the boys came dashing toward the trail.

"Señor...Señorita...por favor." They held out grubby hands.

"Ignore them," Emilio growled. "Once they learn to beg, they won't work. They'll graduate to thievery."

His advice made sense. But as they passed the two ragamuffins, it was all Grace could do to turn her face away. If she'd had money in her pocket, she would have flung it at the young wretches. But there was nothing she could do. Even in this beautiful country, poverty was woven into the landscape.

She needed to know more, to make sense of what she'd just seen. "Emilio?"

He turned at the sound of his name. As he looked at her—then past her—his face froze. "No!" he shouted.

Grace glanced back in time to see one of the boys pull back the rubber on his slingshot and release a thumb-sized rock. The rock sang through the air and whacked into Manso's haunch.

The startled gelding screamed, reared and started to buck. Caught off guard, Grace lost her hold on the reins and lurched partway out of the saddle. Only a death grip on the horse's mane kept her from slamming to the ground.

Hold on! Through a fog of terror, her brain shrilled one command. As Manso broke into a run Grace wrapped her arms around the sturdy neck. Gripping the saddle with her knees, she clung for dear life. Limbs and brush clawed her skin as they tore down the wooded slope.

Was Emilio calling her name? Was he coming up from behind, thundering closer on the big palomino? Or was it only the wind she heard and the pounding of her own heart? To look back would be to risk losing her grip and being dragged or crushed.

The sound of rushing water reached her ears. The river—it had to be close. A plunge over the steep bank could be fatal for both her and the horse. Dared she risk a fall to the ground? But her unyielding grip on Manso's neck answered that question. She was helpless to do anything but hold on.

"Grace!" She heard Emilio's voice and felt the palomino's body pressing in close as he caught her belt. "I've got you! Let go!"

Grace struggled against the instinct to hold on. She had to trust him. Her life depended on it.

"Grace, let go! Do it *now!*" He cursed as he yanked at her waist. Summoning the last of her courage, Grace released her hold on Manso's neck. Emilio jerked her out of the saddle.

One of her sandals had caught in a stirrup. She twisted her bare foot free as Manso veered away from the river and bolted toward home. For a fearful moment she hung from Emilio's arm while he reined the palomino to a halt. Then, as his hold loosened, she slid down the horse's side and dropped to the ground.

"Are you all right?" He let go of the reins and swung out of the saddle.

"I...don't know." Grace was too shaken to stand. She sank to her knees.

Looming over her, he reached down and tilted her chin. His troubled eyes searched her face. "No tears. Is that a good sign or a bad one?"

Grace shook her head. There were no words for how frightened she'd been. But now she felt strangely removed from what had happened, as if she'd just watched a scene from a movie. It felt frightening...but not quite real.

"We need to get you back to the house." His big hands framed her shoulders, lifting her to her feet. "We'll have to ride double. With your shoe gone, there's no way you can walk that far."

Grace stood quivering between his hands, her self-control as fragile as thin ice. With effort, she forced a little laugh and spoke.

"Poor old Manso. He didn't know what hit him. He must've been scared half to death."

Emilio's gaze softened. "Manso will be fine once he calms down. It's you I'm worried about."

"Don't worry. I'll be fine, too." But she wasn't fine now. As the shock wore off, Grace felt herself beginning to crumble. Her skin felt cold. Her chest jerked with dry sobs.

"It's all right, Grace." He gave her a gentle shake. When that had no effect, he muttered a Spanish curse and gathered her close, holding her hard against his chest. "It's all right, *niña*. You're safe now. Go ahead and cry."

Grace closed her eyes and tried to sink into the solid wall of his strength. Tears would have been a release, but they refused to come. She was shaking harder than ever.

"So…sorry," she gasped. "I feel like such a fool…"

"A very brave fool," he murmured, cupping her chin. "And a very beautiful fool."

Grace couldn't really explain what she did next. Her head was still spinning and she felt cold all over…while he looked so warm, so solid and comforting. Before she was even aware she'd moved, she was leaning in and capturing his lips in a kiss.

She couldn't have anticipated the rush of dizzying heat as his lips responded, taking possession of hers. She couldn't have known how it would feel—the deep, throbbing ache as his hands molded her against his rock-hard body—or how much she'd need what this man was giving her.

Unbidden, her arms slid around his neck, binding him close as the kiss went on and on. Moments ago she'd been shaking. Now she was a flaming bonfire.

Five

Emilio ended the kiss, savoring the way their moist lips clung as they parted. He hadn't expected the kiss. But it had happened and, for the moment at least, he wasn't sorry. Grace Chandler's luscious curves fit his body as if they'd been molded for that very purpose. Her sweetness flowed through him like hot caramel syrup over ice cream.

His erection had sprung to readiness. Now, as he cradled her close, the pressure threatened to split the crotch of his jeans. So much for his resolve to treat her like a sister. That wasn't going to happen. He knew himself too well to question his instincts. Sooner or later, damn the consequences, he would have this woman in his bed.

But right now he needed to get her back to the house. She was badly scared, maybe even injured. She might have initiated the kiss, but she was in no condition to take their passion any further. Seduction would have to wait.

With a twinge of regret, he eased her to arm's length. Her

cheeks were flushed, her mouth damp and a little swollen. It was all he could do to keep from snatching her close once more and taking up where they'd left off.

"Are you all right, Grace?" Given the way she looked, it was a needless question.

For a moment she regarded him with lust-glazed eyes. Then a transformation came over her. Straightening her spine and squaring her shoulders she impaled him with a glare that would have done justice to Sister Benedicta, who'd whacked his knuckles in her arithmetic class.

"I'll be fine," she said. "But what just happened was a mistake, Emilio."

He quirked an eyebrow. He refrained from reminding her that she was the one to start the kiss. From the look in her eyes, it would only lead to another whack. Instead, he simply said, "I had the impression you enjoyed it as much as I did."

Her look darkened. "I came here to decide what was best for Zac and for me. The last thing I need is having my judgment clouded by a Latin Romeo who'd hit on any female old enough to drive. As far as you and I are concerned, nothing happened here. Understood?"

"Understood." The barb had stung more than he cared to admit. But long experience had taught Emilio when to advance and when to retreat. This was retreat time. But the conquest was far from over.

Grace Chandler was going to eat her words.

Grace's chest tightened as she eyed Emilio's golden stallion. "I suppose I'll have to get on your horse."

"Unless you want to limp home with one bare foot and what is likely a twisted ankle, yes, it looks that way."

He swung onto the horse, then reached down for her. Feeling as if she were about to mount a fire-breathing dragon, Grace took his hand and allowed him to swing her up behind him. Years ago, riding such a magnificent animal would have thrilled her. Now all she felt was a paralyzing dread. The gentle Manso had started to ease her fear. But their wild plunge down the slope had reawakened the nightmare.

Emilio nudged the stallion to a walk. Its gait was like flowing silk, but she could feel the palomino's dangerous power. When she looked at the ground, Grace felt dizzy. She wrapped her arms around Emilio's ribs and clung.

The contact with his hard-muscled body triggered a gush of memory. Their kiss had burned all the way to the soles of her feet. When his erection swelled against her belly it had been all she could do to keep from rising on tiptoe to press her hunger against him. Even now, the thought of that rock-hard length turned her legs to warm jelly. But if she had any sense she'd blot the sensation from her mind. She'd been on the verge of a foolish mistake—a mistake that mustn't be allowed to happen.

Grace was no stranger to love. Four years ago she'd been engaged to a bookstore owner she'd met through her work. Andrew had been everything she'd ever wanted—caring, sensitive and dependable, a man who treasured family and wanted a houseful of children. At first it hadn't sunk in that he'd have to choose between the woman he loved and his dream of being a father. Only after Grace forced him to face the truth had he made his decision and walked away.

Since then she'd steered clear of romantic involvement. She was damaged goods; and getting her heart broken had hurt too much the first time. As for casual sex, the few times it happened had only left her feeling cheap and unfulfilled. Sleeping with Emilio would be no different—and where Zac was concerned, it would only weaken her position.

She didn't want to be a hired nanny or a live-in mistress. What she wanted was respect and a say in how Zac was to be raised. She wanted to be regarded—and treated—as the boy's mother. If that wasn't possible she would fight with all she had to take him home.

"A penny for your thoughts." He spoke into the silence. "Isn't that what you said to me in the car?"

"I'm not sure my thoughts are worth a penny."

"Are you still afraid of my stallion?"

"Only a little," she lied.

"You said you had an accident with a horse. Would you care to tell me about it?"

She hesitated. Talking about that awful day was always painful.

"I want to understand you, Grace. Knowing what happened would make it easier."

"So how do I go about understanding you, Emilio Santana?" she parried.

"No fair changing the subject. I asked you first."

Grace sighed. "All right. I was fifteen. It was Rodeo Week, and I'd been chosen to carry our riding club's banner in the opening procession. My horse was nursing a stone bruise, so I'd borrowed another—a big bay—from the stable owner. I was waiting to ride into the arena when somebody tossed a string of firecrackers under the horse's belly." Her voice faltered. "The animal went crazy. I was thrown and trampled."

"Ay, diós mio!" Emilio muttered. "You told me you were hurt, but I did not realize it was that bad."

"I was rushed to the hospital with severe internal bleeding. The surgeon on duty saved my life." *Not that he was able to save everything,* Grace added silently. That part was too personal to share.

"I recovered," she said. "But there's more to the story. I spent two weeks in the hospital. By the time I was ready to leave, my mother and the doctor had fallen in love. He was Cassidy's father."

"So that's how you and Cassidy came to be sisters."

"And that's how I came to have Zac."

For the space of a long breath, Emilio was silent. Where her hand rested on his ribs, Grace could feel the steady beat of his heart. "Some things happen for a reason, Grace," he said.

"Do they? After so much pain and tragedy? My mother and stepfather gone? Cassidy gone?" Resolute now, she squared her chin. "That precious little boy is all the family I have left. I won't give him up. I can't."

She felt the rise and fall of his chest. "Zac is all the family I have left, too."

"Surely you'll marry. You can have more children."

"*Quizás*. But none of them will be my brother's son. Arturo was the best of our family—strong and steady and wise, everything I wasn't. He looked after us all."

They emerged from the trees at the back of the property. Manso, still saddled, was grazing next to the stable. Grace's sandal dangled from one of the stirrups.

Emilio halted his horse on the grass. Reaching back, he supported Grace as she slipped to the ground with a sigh of relief. Dismounting, he took the reins and walked beside her

"I need to fly to Lima tomorrow morning," he said. "Some corporate business, papers to sign, assets to transfer. I'll be gone for a few days. That will give you time to settle in before the party."

The party! Grace stifled a groan. She dreaded fancy social gatherings, especially with strangers. Maybe she could just pretend to be sick.

"If you need a gown my driver, Francisco, can take you to the finest shop in Cusco. Our family has an account there."

"So you told me. But if I need a new dress I'll buy it myself, thank you."

"Francisco speaks English," he continued as if she hadn't spoken. "I'll leave instructions for him to be at your disposal."

"I really don't want to impose."

Pausing, he turned her to face him. "Listen to me, Grace. I pay Francisco to be on call. He'll welcome the chance to be useful. As for your imposing, I've turned your whole life upside down, taken you away from your home, your work and your friends. Allow me, at least, to do a few nice things for you in return for all you've sacrificed for me."

His controlling manner roused Grace's defenses. "Get this straight, Emilio. I didn't sacrifice anything for *you*. I came here to be with Zac. And now, if you'll excuse me, I should be getting back to him."

Pulling free, she spun away and headed across the grass toward the stable. She'd taken fewer than a dozen strides when something sharp stabbed the ball of her bare foot. She yelped with surprise and pain.

Emilio dropped the reins and sprinted to her side. "Here, let me look." He dropped to one knee, letting her brace herself against his shoulder while he checked her foot.

"You've stepped on a nasty thorn. It's in deep."

"Can you get it out?" Grace's teeth clenched against the pain.

"I could. But I'd rather do it at the house where we can clean it up and bandage it."

"I don't think I can walk on it."

"No, of course you can't." Without another word he swept her up in his arms. Leaving the horse for the groom, he strode toward the house, carrying her as easily as he might have carried a child.

Grace slid her arms around his neck to ease the weight. Her head rested in the hollow of his throat. Their earlier spat seemed trivial now that she thought of it. "Impressive," she joked. "I'm not exactly a tiny woman."

"So you're impressed, are you? Did you think I'd never lifted anything heavier than a champagne glass?" His lips brushed her hair as he spoke. Through his shirt, his skin smelled of good, clean man sweat. Grace inhaled him into her senses—anything to take her mind off the burning pain.

"I don't know what I was thinking. All I know about you is what I've read in the tabloids. What's the truth?"

"The truth is that I like to play. But there are things I take seriously, like my family and my friends."

"And women?"

He chuckled. "I enjoy them. They enjoy me. And in case you're wondering, I enjoyed kissing you. Like a sip of exquisite wine."

She started sputtering. Did he think she was like those vacuous women he'd dated before, with nothing on her mind but the pleasure of the moment? Or worse, did he think that because she'd kissed him—in a moment of weakness, without considering the consequences—that she was now interested in having a fling?

"That kiss was a mistake," she said, her voice tight and tense. "There's more to life than enjoyment—especially when it's so fleeting. The kiss won't be repeated."

He shrugged gracefully. "As you like. After all, it was just a kiss. No strings attached, as they say. You make too much of simple pleasures, Miss Grace Chandler."

Grace groped for a witty retort but came up empty. What could she say that would make any difference to his outlook? Emilio was all male, unapologetically Latin and raised to a life of excess privilege and minimum responsibility. With that upbringing, it was little surprise that he appeared to view women as toys, slaves or breeding stock. Left in charge, he would likely raise Zac the same way. She couldn't allow that to happen.

"Does your foot hurt much?" His voice was surprisingly tender.

Grace nodded. She'd tried not to think about the injury but it was bad, like a red-hot nail driven into her foot.

"I shouldn't have let you walk on the grass without your shoe. At least it wasn't a scorpion." His arms tightened around her. "Relax, we're almost there."

Nestling her head against his chest, Grace willed herself to take deep breaths and shift her thoughts away from the thorn. What came to mind to distract her was Emilio's kiss. He claimed he'd enjoyed it. Well, heaven help her, so had she. Even now, the memory set off tingles of pleasure in the core of her body. No strings attached, he'd said. Was that an invitation to try it again?

Why was she even considering it? Was pain blurring her common sense? And what had happened to turn her into a whimpering damsel in distress? It wasn't Emilio's job to rescue her. She was supposed to be a strong, self-sufficient woman.

"Here we are." They'd reached the side of the pool. Emilio lowered her to a shaded lounge chair and placed a cushion under her injured foot. "Take it easy. I won't be long."

Grace lay back in the chair as he strode toward the house. The stone waterfall at the pool's far end made soothing music. There was no sign of the handsome young worker she'd glimpsed earlier, which was fine. All she wanted to do was rest and try not to think about her throbbing foot.

She must have drifted off because Emilio seemed to return as quickly as he'd left. The silver tray he carried held tweezers, alcohol, gauze and tape, as well as a bottle of wine, a stemmed crystal glass and a little terra-cotta jar with a wooden stopper. Placing the tray on a side table, he poured dark red wine into the glass. "From the Santana vineyards. Something for you to sip while I doctor your foot."

Grace took the glass. The wine was superb, its flavor a warm tingle on her tongue. Like Emilio's kiss.

"I didn't know you'd be doing this job yourself," she said.

"I doctor the horses when I'm here. Who better?" He glanced up from where he'd crouched at her feet. "You've had a tetanus shot, yes?"

"Yes. Last year." Grace had updated her own immunizations when Zac went for his first shots.

"Good. Here goes. It's liable to hurt."

"Enough of this wine and I won't feel a thing."

He swabbed her foot with alcohol and reached for the tweezers. Grace took another sip of wine, savoring the taste as he bent closer and gripped the thorn with the tweezer tips.

"I'm not—" She gasped. Tears rushed as he eased the thorn out of her flesh.

"Here's the little devil." He held up the tweezers. The thorn looked as vicious as a tiger's fang, with a tiny barb at the tip. "Now you know why it hurt so much. But we'll take care of that now."

He swabbed her foot again, opened the jar and smeared a gooey black poultice onto her wound. "Dolores's uncle brews this up. He's a *curandero*—a healer. Quite the old character—I paid him a visit years ago, and he told me the secrets of living a contented life. I realize now that I should've paid more attention."

"What's in this stuff?" Grace's foot was beginning to numb.

Emilio shrugged. "Pinesap. Burned coca leaves. God knows what else. But it works on horses—dulls the pain, speeds the healing."

He began to wrap the gauze. Grace felt his hands cradling her foot, touching her ankle, his wrist brushing her bare calf. His dark head was bent over her leg, nearly close enough to touch as well. What would he do if she reached out and stroked a fingertip around the edge of his ear? She warmed disturbingly at the thought.

With a restless hand, she raked back her hair. "I need to get back to Zac. Will it be all right for me to walk?"

"If you're careful." He knotted the ends of the gauze and stood. "Zac's down for a nap, so you might as well take it easy. I'll get your shoe." He picked up the empty wineglass she'd set on the tray. "Refill?"

"Just a little."

"Stay here and rest. That's an order." He filled the glass partway, placed it in her hand and strode off toward the stables.

Feeling light-headed, Grace sipped the wine. The pool was a deep, calm blue, the splash of the waterfall as soothing as a lullaby. Gazing at the empty diving board, she imagined Cassidy poised on the end of it, her body slim and flawless in a green bikini, her titian hair glinting in the sunlight. With a backward smile, she raised her arms, made a perfect dive and vanished without a sound beneath the water.

Grace managed to replace the glass on the tray before she sank into sleep.

Emilio returned twenty minutes later with the missing sandal. The errand would have been a simple one, but something had happened at the stables. He'd arrived to find the two horses still saddled and bridled. Fermín, the young groom, was nowhere in sight.

Annoyed, he'd been about to look for the fellow when he heard unmistakable noises coming from the hayloft. Fermín, an aggravatingly handsome lout, was entertaining female company again.

For a moment Emilio had weighed the idea of calling him down on the spot. But he didn't relish humiliating the fool girl, who probably thought she was in love. Instead he had put away the horses himself, departed with a sharp knock on the ceiling, and resolved to fire the worthless groom at the end of the day. Fermín had been warned before about letting dalliances interfere with his duties, as had his older brother Pablo, who cut the grass and cleaned the pool. Both of them were so handsome that women of all classes fell into their beds. But if they couldn't keep their pants zipped at work, it was time they found a more lenient employer or took up new careers as gigolos.

He'd picked up Grace's sandal and returned to the pool, where he'd found her asleep. Now he stood gazing down at her, thinking he ought to leave her in peace. Instead, feeling strangely protective, he pulled up a lightweight chair and sat nearby.

With her eyes closed and her sun-kissed hair tumbling around her face she looked as vulnerable as a child. He'd known many women more beautiful than Grace Chandler, but never one whose true nature seemed so close to the surface. He'd found no artifice in her, no charm or gaiety that masked a conniving soul. She was who she was—fiercely loyal, loving, outspoken and tender.

His gaze lingered on her full lips. Remembering the taste of her mouth, Emilio felt his body warm and stir. The temptation to bend over her and brush those lips with his was nearly irresistible. But he held himself in check. She'd called their kiss a mistake. She would no doubt take offense if she knew it was a mistake he intended to repeat. Best to wait until he'd had longer to persuade her to his way of thinking.

Pouring wine into the glass she'd emptied, he settled back into the chair. He was beginning to drift when Eugenia appeared from the house. She carried a grumpy-looking Zac in her arms.

"I think this baby wants his mama," she said in Spanish. "He won't stop fussing, and *Tía* Dolores needs us in the kitchen."

As if on cue, Zac spotted Grace. "Mama!" he cooed, reaching out with his chubby hands.

Emilio sighed. Grace was sleeping so peacefully that it seemed a shame to wake her. He held out his arms. "Give me the boy. I'll keep him until she wakes up."

Clearly relieved, the maid thrust the squirming baby toward him and fled. Emilio gathered Zac onto his lap. The child eyed him suspiciously, his lower lip jutting outward.

Emilio had no memory of ever having held a baby before. The sensation was unsettling. But he would try to make the best of it. He made an effort to smile.

"Well, Zac, here we are," he said in English. "I suppose it's time you and your uncle Emilio got acquainted."

Six

The child on Emilio's lap didn't look happy. But at least he seemed curious. He stared up at Emilio with chocolate-drop eyes, one finger creeping to his mouth.

"It's all right, boy," Emilio muttered. "I won't hurt you. Look, there's your mother right there." Not that Grace was really the boy's mother. But the words were true in every way that mattered.

"Mama!" Zac strained against Emilio's clasp, reaching for Grace, who remained fast asleep.

"Shhh…" Emilio bounced the tot on his knee, trying to distract him. "Be still. *Déjala en paz.*"

Zac's lower lip slid out another fraction of an inch. His brows crinkled, a warning that a storm was about to break.

Now what? Emilio scrambled for a diversion and found one.

"How would you like to see my horses, Zac?" Rising, he strode out across the grass with Zac in his arms. Zac seemed to like the motion. He gurgled and chatted, reaching up to tug at Emilio's ear.

The three mares had seen them coming and were clustered by the fence. Emilio slowed his approach. He didn't want the boy to be frightened. But he needn't have worried. At the sight of the big animals, Zac began to bounce and jabber. His hand stretched out to touch the white blaze on the nearest mare's face.

The mare sneezed, spraying him with moisture. Zac giggled with delight.

A surge of pride caught Emilio off guard. This bright, fearless little boy already shared his love of horses. "Well done, Zac," he murmured. "I can tell you're a real Santana!"

Grace opened her eyes and sat up. As her confusion cleared she remembered the thorn, the wine and Emilio wrapping her foot. She remembered the wild dash on Manso—and she remembered kissing Emilio.

Where was Emilio now?

Struggling to her feet, she saw him in the distance by the paddock fence. He was holding Zac next to the mares. Her pulse lurched. Her nerves screamed danger for her precious boy. But no, she realized, the scene was peaceful. Even from a distance she could tell that Zac was safe and unafraid in his uncle's arms.

Emotions warred as she watched them. Wasn't this what she'd wanted—for Emilio to start acting like a father to Zac? Now it appeared to be happening. So why did she feel threatened?

A jab of pain reminded her of her injured foot. She sank onto the seat of the lawn chair. Her shoulders sagged as the truth struck her like a belly blow. Zac belonged here, in this place, with this man who was his blood kin. Unless she stayed—perhaps even *if* she stayed—she was destined to lose him.

Emilio had noticed her sitting up. Now he strode back across the grass, bouncing Zac in his arms as if he'd been around children all his life. And Zac was loving it. She could hear him giggling as they came closer.

"Well, he seems to like horses," Emilio said. "When he's big enough, I'll get him a pony of his own."

Grace rose to face him. "The pony can wait a few years. Right now he's still a baby. And if anything happens to him around those horses, so help me, I'll never forgive you." She couldn't stop the warning from slipping out. No matter how much Zac seemed to like the horses, accidents could still happen. "Now if you'll excuse me, I'll take him to my room and get us both cleaned up before lunch."

Holding out her arms for the baby, she moved toward him. The pressure on her bandaged foot shot pain up her leg. She winced, stumbling.

Emilio steadied her with his free arm. "Here, lean on me. I can carry Señor Zac. And I'll arrange for lunch to be brought to your room so you can rest."

"Thank you." Grace clung to his arm, easing the weight on her foot. It wasn't supposed to be this way, she thought. She was supposed to be the strong one. Why did *the Peruvian Playboy* have to be so capable? And why did she have to be so pathetically needy?

They reached her room partway down the long corridor. The bed, which she'd made up hastily that morning, had been smoothed, her travel clothes collected for the laundry. One of the wardrobes had been moved aside to reveal the door behind it. Beyond the doorway was a charming little nursery with lace curtains and storybook figures on the walls. Zac's crib had been moved inside, his clothes and other necessities neatly stored in a cabinet.

"The nursery room hasn't been used since I was a baby," Emilio said. "But I thought you might rest more comfortably if Zac had a room of his own."

Grace gazed around the nursery. It was perfect for Zac. With the door open, she'd be able to hear him when he needed her. She ought to be beaming with gratitude. But it was just one more instance of everything being taken care of for her. It was frustrating. She didn't need servants to see to her things or arrange Zac's room—if they'd let her, she could do it herself. But she couldn't say that, not when Emilio was clearly proud of himself for being thoughtful and considerate.

"So this was *your* nursery," she said. "Was it Arturo's, too?"

"It was. Zac is sleeping in his father's crib."

"So I'm sleeping in your parents' room? In their bed?"

"This was my mother's room. My father slept…elsewhere."

"They were separated?"

"No. It was just the way of things. She valued her privacy. He valued his freedom." He lowered Zac into the crib. "My mother was a beautiful woman. You'll see her portrait in the dining room." He glanced around the room as if seeing things that were no longer present—the clothes, the jewelry, the perfumes, perhaps. "You're the first person to stay in this room since she died."

Grace suppressed a shiver. Perhaps this was the downside of a family home full of history and tradition—ghosts of the past lingered in every room. "Do you suppose she'd mind our being here?"

A look of melancholy, like the shadow of a cloud, passed over Emilio's face. "I imagine she'd be very pleased to have a grandchild in this nursery," he said.

Emilio didn't see Grace again until dinnertime. He'd shut himself in the office and forced himself to go over the books for the estate and the winery, focusing on needless expenses that could be trimmed. He was surprisingly good at the work, but that didn't mean he enjoyed it. Sooner or later, he groused, it would make an old man of him. Being in charge of the Santana holdings was fifty percent stress and fifty percent drudgery. And occasionally, it was both at once.

He hadn't enjoyed firing the errant groom, Fermín, tonight, especially when he'd whined and begged to keep his job. But it had to be done. One more peccadillo, which was bound to happen, and his brother Pablo would be gone, too. Emilio planned to replace the *malcriados* with responsible married men who needed the work to support their families. One more headache Arturo would have taken care of if he'd been here.

The last thing Emilio had expected was for Arturo's Porsche to overshoot a curve on that rain-slicked mountain road. Emilio hadn't been close to his brother in the last few years as their lives had become increasingly separate. But now he missed Arturo's wisdom and common sense. He'd give anything to have him back.

Life took strange turns, he mused. If Arturo hadn't died, Grace would be in Arizona finalizing Zac's adoption. Emilio would likely be partying in some exotic resort or walking the red carpet at a gala movie premiere. The two would never have met.

Now, as he changed his clothes for dinner, Emilio found himself looking forward to seeing her again. Grace Chandler was unlike any woman he'd ever been attracted to—no games, no pretense, just simple honesty.

Their kiss still sizzled in his memory. She'd felt so natural in his arms, so strong, yet needing his comfort. Would he get a chance at a second kiss? *Ojalá.* He looked forward to finding out.

Tonight the long dining room table was set for just two.

But Emilio had requested a full course dinner with candles, flowers and the best china and silver laid out on the linen cloth. Seated at the head of the table, he glanced at his watch. It was five minutes past nine. What if she'd changed her mind about joining him?

Another five minutes passed. He was about to send someone to look for her when she rushed into the room. Dressed in a black sleeveless dress and gold sandals to accommodate her bandaged foot, she looked fresh and adorably flustered.

"I got lost on the way," she said. "Sorry, I don't like to keep people waiting."

"I'm the one who should apologize." Emilio rose, half giddy with relief at the sight of her. "I should've sent someone to escort you."

"No, it's all right. I found the kitchen and Dolores pointed me this way." She stared at the table, her hazel eyes widening. "There's just the two of us?"

"Who else?" He pulled out her chair and seated her. The scent of her freshly washed hair crept into his nostrils—nothing more than ordinary shampoo, but the effect on him was strangely erotic. The modest V-neck of the dress showed a hint of cleavage, just enough to raise the heat in his loins.

Diablos, but he wanted her. He wanted to fling her on the table, yank up that sweet little dress and have his way with her before the first course arrived.

But he was first and foremost a gentleman—or so he told himself. And anyway, he wanted her to want him back—to show him once more that fire and heat he'd felt when she'd kissed him before.

"But this is like a formal banquet," she protested, eyeing the flowers and candles. "Do you do this every night?"

"Only for special guests." He seated himself, enjoying her amazement.

"Then I expect something more ordinary tomorrow. Although I have to say, it's nice eating after the baby's bed-time—but that reminds me. Zac usually sleeps through the night, but I can't stay here long. He might wake up, and I for-got to pack his baby monitor. Can I buy one in this country?"

"I'm sure I can find you one in Lima." What the devil was a baby monitor? He'd have to ask someone at the office.

"How is your foot?" he asked.

"Better. No more pain, even when I walk on it. You should package that black goo and market it in the U.S."

"Something tells me your FDA would never approve it."

"Too bad." The salad had arrived, fresh organic vegetables from the estate gardens. It was a pleasure watching a hungry, healthy female eat—unlike the weight-obsessed models he'd dated, who barely picked at their food.

"I can't believe an attractive woman like you isn't mar-ried," he said.

A hint of shadow crossed her face. "Marriage isn't for ev-eryone. I was engaged a few years ago. It didn't work out."

"I'm sorry."

"No pity needed. I've been happy on my own, especially with…Zac."

Emilio hadn't missed the catch in her voice. He was just beginning to realize how much the baby's loss would devas-tate her. All the more reason to convince her to stay.

"The boy calls you Mama," he said. "I heard him this morning."

"It was his first word." She speared a piece of mango with her fork. "But he'll learn the truth in time, won't he?"

"Grace—"

"Never mind." Her smile was brittle. "Why spoil such a lovely dinner?"

The salad was followed by delicate braised sea bass with roasted and seasoned vegetables. Grace savored each bite, willing herself to focus on the food, and not her disturbingly handsome dinner companion.

"Is your fish good?" Emilio's voice was a velvet caress as he refilled her glass with sparkling white wine.

"*Exquisite* is a better word. Maybe I should ask Dolores to give me cooking lessons."

"Whatever you like." His formal tone hinted that her request might not be welcomed in the kitchen. So much for that topic of conversation. Grace's gaze wandered upward to a life-size painting on the wall behind him. The woman in the portrait looked to be about thirty, petite and slender with upswept black hair and dark eyes so full of fire that they appeared to be alive. Dressed in simple white, with a spectacular emerald necklace, she looked as glamorous as an old-time Hollywood star.

"Your mother, I take it?"

"Yes."

"She's a goddess."

Was his gesture a nod or a shrug? "She was quite the beauty in her day."

"How long has she been gone?" Grace asked.

"Ten years, more or less. She'd requested to be buried in that emerald necklace—a family heirloom that was supposed to bring bad luck. In her case, it did."

"I'd like to know more about her. After all, she's Zac's grandmother, and I'm sleeping in her bed." Grace's hand crept to her throat as a grim possibility struck her. "Oh, no, she didn't—"

"Didn't die in that bed?" His voice was flat with irony. "No, you needn't be concerned. She died in Lima, in somebody else's bed, actually."

"Oh." She stared at him, stunned by his frankness.

"Her beauty was everything to her," he said. "When it began to fade she…" The words trailed off. "Never mind. It isn't a pretty story. My parents weren't what you'd call contented people."

And what about you, Emilio? Grace wanted to ask. But she held her tongue. This playboy dated the world's most glamorous women, but he'd shown no sign of wanting a wife and family. Maybe she'd just glimpsed part of the reason. What did he know about a strong marriage or a close-knit family? His parents certainly hadn't been much of an example, and from the tabloids, it seemed that nothing like true romance had ever come into Emilio's adult life.

No wonder he was so determined to take in Zac. Having a convenient heir would free Emilio from having to find a wife he didn't know how to love. And with that rationale…she couldn't see any reason why he would ever want to let Zac go.

Grace put down her fork. She had lost her appetite.

"What is it?" Emilio was watching her with a concerned expression. "Did I say something wrong?"

Grace pushed her chair back from the table and stood. "Forgive me, I'm suddenly…not feeling well. I need to get back to Zac."

He'd risen with her. "You're upset. If you'll just tell me—"

"No, sit down. I'll be fine in the morning." She fled into the hall, limping on the foot that had suddenly begun to throb again. She knew her behavior was ill-mannered, but all she wanted was to get away. The more time she spent with him, the more she understood his position, which only served to undermine her own.

"Grace!" She heard the scrape of his chair on the tiles.

"Come back here! Whatever's bothering you, we can talk it out!"

He was coming after her. There was no way she could outrun him, but the last thing she wanted tonight was a confrontation. She was tired and emotional. There was too much danger of her saying the wrong thing.

His footsteps were coming closer. Rounding a blind corner in the dimly lit hallway she flattened herself against the wall. Heart pounding, she waited.

He stopped a few feet short of where she stood. Grace could sense his frustration. "I know you're close enough to hear me," he said. "So listen to what I have to say. I know it's been hard on you, having me show up and take Zac away when the adoption was almost final. You probably see me as some kind of despot, and I can't say I blame you. But I didn't ask for my brother to die. I didn't ask to become the last Santana male."

He paused, waiting, perhaps for her reply. When it didn't come, he continued. "All I'm trying to do is what's best for my family and for my brother's son."

"And what about me?" The words burst out before Grace could stop them. She stepped into his sight. "Cassidy gave me her baby to raise. I'm the only parent Zac knows. I love him more than anything else in this world. Doesn't that count for something?"

In the dim light, Emilio's face looked drawn and weary. "I've seen your love for him, Grace. You're a wonderful mother. But Arturo will never father another child. You can have more children—your own children."

"No, I can't!" She battled unshed tears. "The accident I told you about, with the horse. I was…damaged internally. The doctors made it perfectly clear. There's no way I'll ever be able to have a baby."

He made a low sound. "Grace, I'm so sorry."

"I could try to adopt again, but for a single woman that might take years. And even if it were to happen, that child wouldn't be Zac. I've had him since the day he was born. He's in my heart forever, no matter what happens. You've never loved a child. You have no idea what a mother feels."

She wasn't sure how it happened, but suddenly he'd gathered her close and was cradling her in his arms. Grace felt the fight drain out of her. Resting her head against his chest, she listened to the steady pulsing of his heart. His strength felt like something she'd needed for longer than she could remember.

He muttered a curse in Spanish. "You might have told me."

"Would you have acted any differently?" How could she feel such resentment and such need at the same time?

"At least it might have kept me from sounding like an insensitive fool. I would have made it clearer that you don't have to give Zac up. I want you to stay, Grace. I want you to raise the boy here in Peru."

"But not as his legal mother." She pushed away and stood glaring up at him. "He'd be *your* heir, not *my* child. I'd be nothing more than a glorified nanny who could be dismissed at a moment's notice."

"You really believe I'd do that to you? To Zac?" he demanded.

"Right now? No. In a few years, when he doesn't need me as much? Perhaps."

He shook his dark head. "You must see me as some kind of monster."

"Not a monster. Just a manipulative, self-serving man who is accustomed to satisfying his desires at any cost."

Emilio's hands flashed, moving to her shoulders, gripping hard. When he spoke his voice was a low growl. "You know nothing of my desires, or how hard I fight against them. I'm trying to treat you honorably, Grace. I would advise you not to push me."

Recklessness stole over her, and she shifted in his grip enough to move closer. "And if I told you I didn't believe in your honor…what then?"

"In that case, I'd have nothing to lose."

His arms jerked her against him. His rough kiss was predatory, burning through her body like a blowtorch. Grace's pulse—already heightened—broke into a thundering gallop. For the space of a breath she struggled. Then a rush of heat compelled her to respond. Her torso molded to his, soft breast to muscled chest, hip to straining hip. As the kiss triggered freshets of pleasure, her arms crept around his neck. Her frantic fingers furrowed his hair. The smell and taste and feel of him was heaven. All she wanted was more.

He groaned as her mouth opened to his tongue's probing invasion. She felt each thrust and retreat as a sensual pantomime of what they both wanted. If she didn't stop them…

But she *had* to stop, the voice of caution whispered. If for no other reason than that the middle of the hallway was no place for this to continue.

Somehow she found the strength to tear herself loose. Disheveled and trembling, she faced him. "We can't do this. Not here and definitely not now. I need to get back to Zac. He could be waking up."

"Of course." For an instant he almost looked vulnerable. Then his mouth twitched in a knowing smile. "But since you were running in the wrong direction, you'll have a long walk back to him on your sore foot. Allow me."

With that he swept her up in his arms. Any hopes she'd had of regaining her self-control and banishing her desire vanished. In spite of herself, she relaxed into his arms, letting herself relish their strength and the wonderful way they felt wrapped around her body.

Powerful strides carried her back down the hallway toward her room. Grace's head lay against his chest. His voice rumbled in her ear as he spoke.

"You're a beautiful woman, Grace Chandler—so warm and so passionate. Making love to you would be a pleasure for both of us. So why do I sense such resistance in you?"

Because I have to think about tomorrow and the day after and all the days to come...

The words were there, inside Grace's head. But the power to speak them, or even fully believe was gone, lost in the wild drumming of her heart. Desire, hot and sweet, flooded her body. She felt herself trembling, but she wanted this. She needed this. It was going to happen.

Seven

The scent of jasmine drifted through the shutters as Emilio lowered Grace's feet to the floor. Touching a finger to his lips, she took a moment to slip into the nursery.

Zac lay in the crib, sprawled in angelic sleep. Bending over him, she brushed a finger down his rose petal cheek. For the past eleven months she'd lived her whole life for this precious little boy. Tonight wouldn't change anything, she vowed. Whatever happened between her and Emilio, Zac would always come first.

But Zac clearly didn't need her right now. And Emilio was waiting.

Easing the door shut behind her, she returned to the bedroom. Emilio was standing by the bed, his feet bare, his black linen shirt unbuttoned to the waist. He had turned on the bedside lamp.

Could she really do this? Would she regret it more if she did—or if she didn't?

He opened his arms. "You're thinking too hard," he said. "Come here, Grace."

She remembered the ugly scar. "Could you turn off the light?"

"But why? I want to see you. I want to watch your beautiful face as I pleasure you."

"Please, Emilio."

He did as she'd asked. Now only moonlight, filtering through the shutters, softened the darkness. "Now come." His whisper was a caress. "Come to me."

He met her partway across the floor, his strong arms enfolding her, pulling her close. A tremor passed through her body as his lips brushed her face, skimming her temple, her eyelids, her earlobes, in a teasing dance that ended as he claimed her mouth. His kiss sent her over the edge.

Heat rushed through her veins. Sliding her hands into his open shirt, she pulled it away from his body, baring his skin to her touch. Her lips escaped his to trail down his throat to his chest. He groaned out loud as her tongue circled one taut nipple.

"*Ay,* what are you doing to me, woman? Whatever you have in mind, don't stop."

She drew the tiny, swollen nub between her lips. The taste of him was sweet and clean and salty. Emilio's breath roughened as his fingers found the hem of her dress and rucked it over her hips. His hand pulled her hips against the long, hard bulge of his erection.

"I've been wanting to get under that little black dress all night," he muttered, sliding it higher. "Now all I can think about is getting it off you." He released her long enough to pull the light knit dress over her head and toss it aside. Pulling her close again, he buried his face in the cleft between her breasts. One expert hand loosened the front clasp of her bra. "You feel so good…so good…" he murmured, nibbling the tender flesh that had fallen free of the black lace cups. "I want you, Grace. I want to enjoy all of you."

Her panties shifted downward, dropping around her ankles as his fingertip found her moisture-slicked entrance. His delicate strokes triggered ripples of unspeakable pleasure, mounting, growing until she came, gasping and thrusting against his hand.

Emilio chuckled as she sagged against him. "More?"

"More," she breathed.

"*Un momento.* Show me how much you want it."

Aching with need, Grace arched against his arousal. Her hands ranged over his body, savoring the hardness of his muscles and the warmth of his golden skin. Heaven save her, she couldn't get enough of him.

The crisp, black hair that dusted his chest narrowed to form a trail from sternum to belly. She traced it downward with a fingertip, pausing at his belt buckle.

"Don't stop now," he whispered. "I want to feel your hand holding me."

Grace's pulse skittered as his trousers and briefs fell away. Cradled in her palm, he felt as big as a stallion, thrilling to the touch. Her fingers tightened around his shaft, eliciting a low groan. She wanted this man—wanted him so much that she was ready for him the moment they tumbled into the bed.

"Now!" she whispered as he took a moment to don protection, then mounted between her legs. "Please, I can't wait…"

Clearly Emilio felt the same. Finding her moist opening he pushed home—no games now, no pretty words, just a man with an urgent need. His length filled her as he drove in deep and hard. Her legs clasped his pounding hips as she met his thrusts, whimpering with each surge of hot sensation. He was lost in her now, each push carrying him closer to his peak. She rode the wave with him, feeling his powerful breath, his tightening muscles and the low grunt of release. Their joined climax rocked her, shaking her to the roots of her being.

She cradled him close as, with a long sigh, he relaxed against her. "That was lovely," she whispered.

"Was?" He chuckled in her ear. "You speak as if we were finished. Don't you know we're just getting started?"

Easing his weight to one side, he pressed a tender kiss on her mouth, then grazed his way down her throat to her breasts. Taking his time, he let his mouth toy with each nipple, sucking with his lips, teasing with his tongue until Grace felt the hot tightening of her loins. Unbelievably, after her shattering climax, she was fully aroused once more. Unbidden, her hips moved, butting playfully against him.

"Ay, so soon, woman?" He laughed softly. "I am not a god, you know. A man needs time—but when I am with one as lovely as you, only a little as you shall see."

His nibbling caresses moved down the midline between her ribs, lingered a moment, then skimmed her navel. She stiffened as his lips brushed the ridge of the scar that crossed her belly from hip to hip.

"So this is from your accident," he murmured.

Grace managed a nervous laugh. "Now you know why I wanted the light off."

"Hush." He kissed the ugly line. "A woman's scars tell the story of her suffering—and her strength. You are a strong woman, Grace, and every inch of you is beautiful."

His tantalizing mouth moved downward, past the scar. A moan escaped her lips as he parted her labia, opening her like the petals of a rose. The first brush of his tongue against her delicate center created a shimmer of ecstasy through her body. She gasped. Her hands caught his hair, holding him in place as she came again, then again in a firestorm of wild sensations.

As she released him he smiled in the darkness. "What

a woman you are. If you haven't had enough, I believe I'm ready for you again."

Grace laughed with pure sensual pleasure. "I'll let you know when I've had enough. Come here."

Birdcalls woke Grace at first light. Emilio was gone, as she'd known he would be. What man would want to face a tired, rumpled woman after a night like the one he'd given her?

Aching pleasantly in unaccustomed places, she stretched out on her back. She felt deliciously wicked. She'd made love with the staid, traditional Andrew before their breakup, but last night had been a revelation—like riding a comet into space. She would never be the same again.

No strings attached. At least Emilio had been honest with her. She'd known better than to expect commitment from him, let alone love. The man had promised pleasure and he'd delivered it. She'd be naive to ask for anything more.

But what would be the state of things when he returned from Lima? Would he act as if nothing had happened? Or worse, would he expect free access to her bed whenever he felt the urge? They'd never actually discussed whether "no strings attached" meant "one time only." Would he think she'd signed on to become his live-in mistress?

She shivered at the thought, partially in dismay and partially in reluctant pleasure. Last night had been phenomenal. And she was sure that any additional lovemaking they shared would be equally pleasurable. But what would be the cost?

How could she stand up to Emilio after what had happened? How could she keep his respect when it came to decisions about Zac?

It would be different if the previous night had started a real relationship—one based on emotional as well as physical intimacy. But a real relationship was impossible with

Emilio. An independent, stubborn and—most shockingly—barren American woman would never suit anyone's picture of a proper Peruvian wife. She could never be more than his mistress. She'd have to remember that, and make certain that she kept her heart protected, no matter what. Only then could she be certain she was doing what was best for herself and for Zac.

Zac was stirring in the next room. She could hear the creak of the crib frame as he pulled himself up. Before long he'd be big enough to climb out.

"Mama!" The sound of his voice went straight to her heart. Flinging on her robe, Grace hurried into the nursery. Zac was standing in the crib, doing pull-ups on the rail. His face lit in a baby-toothed grin when he saw her.

"Good morning, big boy!" Lifting him in her arms, she nuzzled the sweet spot on the side of his neck. He smelled of sleep and milk and a diaper that needed changing. Love flooded her as she held him close. Whatever the law decreed, Zac was hers in a way that he could never be anyone else's.

She'd been there at his birth and had seen him through eleven months of life. No one could take that away, and no one could keep her from protecting him—not even Emilio.

Emilio hadn't set foot in the family's Lima penthouse since his brother's death. Arturo had lived there whenever business kept him in town. Over the years, the place had become a second home to him, one that Emilio had frequently visited.

Now, as he unlocked the door with his brother's key, Emilio braced himself for a flood of memories. He'd considered hiring someone to clear out the suite of rooms. But only he would know which items to keep and which to discard. A few personal things, like photos and letters, would be worth saving for Zac. These he would box up and take home. But the clothes and other items with no sentimental value could be donated to charity.

Arturo had been obsessively neat. Only small human touches—the cashmere robe flung over a chair, the open book on a nightstand, the crumpled tube of toothpaste in the bathroom and the kidskin slippers tossed under the bed—disturbed the sense of perfect order.

The walk-in closet was less than half-full. Emilio glanced at the custom tailored Italian suits, the silk ties, the designer shirts and immaculately polished shoes. He would donate all the clothes to charity, including the diamond cuff links and the vicuña overcoat that was worth a king's ransom. The state-of-the-art stereo and wall-sized high-definition TV could go, as well.

For his own use, Emilio would have the suite stripped down to bare essentials. Stripped of ghosts, memories and regrets. Or maybe he could just put the place up for sale and buy something smaller. It wasn't as if he planned on spending a lot of time in town. With some technical updates, like a bigger satellite dish, he'd be able to do most of his conferencing from the Urubamba estate. That would certainly suit him better. But would limiting his time in Lima damage the business relationships Arturo had built in the area? Emilio didn't know. As with so many things relating to the family business, he would have to learn everything from the beginning, struggling with trial and error.

If only things had been different between him and his brother. Arturo had loved him, but that love had never truly been paired with respect. Like most people, he'd seen Emilio as a ne'er-do-well who could not be relied upon. He'd never bothered trying to instruct Emilio in any of their business ventures. Would that ever have changed, had he lived? Emilio didn't know. An unlucky spin on a slippery road had closed that door forever.

Now fate had given Emilio a second chance to prove himself, even if only to his brother's memory. But there was an even greater concern than the business affairs; a legacy far more important left behind by his brother into Emilio's care. Could he raise Arturo's son to be a good and honorable man? Could he become the kind of father he and Arturo had never known?

He didn't know the first thing about parenting. But with Grace at his side he could learn. She was so loving and patient with the boy. There were many things she could teach him.

Grace. His last glimpse of her this morning lingered in Emilio's memory—sun-pale hair tangled on the pillow, satin lips, swollen from his kisses, eyes closed in exhausted slumber. She was beautiful and passionate, but more than that, she was a simple, honest, loving woman. Was that what he'd needed all along?

With so many other concerns this morning, he'd tried to put her out of his thoughts. But she'd been there all along, like an anchor on a storm-battered ship. He would get back to her, he vowed. The two of them were due for some serious conversation—if they could keep their hands off each other long enough to talk.

Meanwhile he needed to finish going through the apartment today. Starting tomorrow, he had meetings scheduled with the boards of the various Santana companies. The meetings would last for the remainder of the week, allowing him just enough time to make it home for the Saturday night party.

He saved Arturo's desk for last. The computer and printer would be kept, of course, as would the basic office supplies stored in the drawers. Still, he'd need to make a mental inventory of what was here.

With a weary sigh, he opened the bottom right drawer. It was filled with paper, empty manila folders and what appeared to be a stack of computer manuals. He'd slipped his hand beneath the manuals and was lifting them out when he felt a sharp jab.

Emilio muttered a curse and jerked his hand away. The cut on his index finger was deep enough to drip blood. After stanching the flow with a bandage from the bathroom, he returned to the open drawer. This time he removed the manuals with more care. Underneath the stack was an eight-by-ten-inch photo in a silver frame. Its glass was cracked into jagged pieces as if by a sharp blow.

Dumping the glass shards into the wastebasket, Emilio stared at the photo beneath. It was a stunning black-and-white close-up of Cassidy, laughing as she pushed her wind-rumpled hair back from her sunlit face.

Arturo had seemed so happy when Cassidy was with him. Had they quarreled? Had she broken off the relationship, perhaps because she knew she was dying?

Replacing the photo, Emilio closed the drawer. What had made Arturo angry enough to smash the glass—and why hadn't he destroyed the photograph behind it? The natural conclusion was that he'd loved Cassidy and she'd hurt him. But he would never know for sure. The truth had died with his brother that black night on a wet mountain road.

Grace sidestroked her way across the pool, savoring the silky coolness of water on her skin. In Emilio's absence, she'd grown to enjoy these afternoon dips. With Ana and Eugenia clamoring to watch Zac, she found herself with unaccustomed free time. Lap swimming helped keep her in shape and burned up nervous energy.

When Emilio returned from the capital, she would remind him about the promised studio space. It was high time she started working again.

Her pulse quickened at the thought of Emilio's return.

They'd spent a wonderful night together, but she knew better than to assume anything about their future relationship. A man like Emilio could have glamorous women falling into his bed every night of the week—especially in a big city like Lima. She imagined him partying, nightclubbing, hooking up with Peruvian beauties…

Grace brought herself up with a mental slap. What was wrong with her? Was she actually jealous? This had to stop right now.

Much as she'd enjoyed her night with Emilio, did she want to continue their "no strings attached" arrangement? How could she sacrifice her self-respect and settle for being just one of his women?

Taking a breath, she plunged underwater and flutter-kicked the full length of the pool. She surfaced, gasping, at the far end, to find herself looking at a pair of muscular, suntanned legs.

Her startled eyes moved upward to lean hips clad in low-slung khaki shorts, a bare, bronzed chest and the face of a youthful Adonis crowned by shoulder-length curls. Only as the surprise wore off did Grace realize she was seeing the young man who tended the pool.

"Hello." His smile revealed flawless white teeth. "You are *Doña* Grace, yes? I hear about a beautiful woman. Now I meet a goddess."

Grace suppressed a giggle. Did this overly confident boy expect her to fall for his silly pickup line?

He extended his hand. "My name is Pablo, *a tu servicio.* Allow me to help you out of the water. I have a warm towel and a Pisco Sour waiting by your chair."

"A Pisco Sour, you say?" Grace had heard of the Peruvian cocktail, but had never seen or tasted one. "That's very kind of you, but I'm not much of a drinker."

"But you must try it. The Pisco is from the finest grapes

grown here in the Sacred Valley. They mix it with *limón* and the foam of an egg white. The taste is *exquisito!* And I make this one just for you, beautiful lady."

Grace's first impulse was to swim to the far end of the pool and make her escape, but she was getting cold and Pablo had mentioned a warm towel. The fellow seemed harmless enough. Why not chat with him for a few minutes?

Reaching up, she allowed him to help her out of the pool. The ample white towel he held out for her had indeed been warmed. Grace wrapped herself in its delicious heat.

"And now the Pisco Sour. If you will sit, *por favor.*"

Grace curled in the chair. The drink he handed her was a pale green-gold, topped with a layer of white foam. She sipped it cautiously, feeling the slight buzz on her tongue.

Taking a seat, Pablo watched her from across the small table. "It is the national drink of my country. You like?"

"It's…different." Grace took another sip and set the glass down. There appeared to be something on his mind, and whatever it was, she wanted to get the conversation over with. "Is there something you want from me, Pablo?"

"Only to know you. And to ask maybe a small favor."

So there it was. "What kind of favor?" Grace asked.

"*Don* Emilio is in Lima, yes?"

"Yes, he said he'd be back before the party this weekend. Why?"

"*Don* Emilio is your friend, yes?"

"I suppose so." Grace felt a pinprick of suspicion. "What's this about?"

Pablo's beautiful eyes were dark wells of melancholy. "It is about my poor brother, Fermín. He has worked in the stable almost three years—a faithful worker, my brother. But two days ago, *Don* Emilio fired him—for nothing. And I fear that soon he will fire me *también.*"

"And you want me to try and change his mind."

He seized Grace's hand in an intimate clasp. "I would not ask for myself, *Doña* Grace. It is for our poor mama! She needs money for her medicine. We must have work!"

Grace tugged at her hand, liking the situation less and less. "Listen to me, Pablo. I'm only a guest here. I have no influence with *Don* Emilio."

"But you do. You are a beautiful woman. He likes beautiful women. If you offer to—"

"Oh, for heaven's sake!" Yanking her hand free, Grace rose. "I'm sorry about your mother, Pablo, but I'm in no position to help you."

Pablo stood, his charming mask stripped away. "*Muy bien.* I will not ask a second time. But let me leave you with a warning. *Don* Arturo was a good man. He had a kind heart. But *Don* Emilio, he has no heart at all. He cares only for his parties and his women. If you fall in love with him, *querida,* you will be one of many. And in the end you will be sorry. Very sorry."

With that parting salvo, he turned and stalked away. Grace stood looking after him, shivering under the towel that was no longer warm.

Eight

Grace checked her reflection in the tall dresser mirror. How many generations of Santana women had done the same? she mused as she adjusted an earring. Could a mirror hold images, trapped like ghosts beneath its glassy surface? Could their disapproving eyes be looking back at her, sight unseen?

Shaking off the grim notion, she stepped back for a final turn before the mirror. The cream-colored silk cocktail dress she'd bought in Cusco, using her own credit card, would do nicely for the party. The bodice, with its thin spaghetti straps, was cut to display her tanned shoulders without revealing too much skin. The bands of gold embroidery that circled the hem matched her gypsy hoop earrings and strappy high-heeled sandals. Her hair was loosely twisted and clipped at the crown of her head. She looked fine, Grace assured herself. But her stomach was a knot of dread. A den of hungry tigers would be less daunting than what she was about to face.

From somewhere down the hall, a clock struck eight. Party

time. But should she wait to be summoned or blunder down the hall toward the light and music?

Emilio had arrived earlier that afternoon—the new baby monitor, delivered to her room by Eugenia, confirmed that he was home. But Grace had yet to see him, and she had no idea what to expect. The uncertainty was even worse than the prospect of walking into a room full of strangers.

She could get undressed, crawl into bed and pretend to be sick. But something told her Emilio wouldn't be fooled.

Her thoughts were interrupted by a light rap on the door. She opened it to find him standing on the threshold. Dressed in an open-collared black shirt and a tailored raw silk dinner jacket, he looked every inch the billionaire playboy.

His gaze roamed up and down her body. "You look delicious. Are you ready?"

"Would it make any difference if I wasn't?"

His grin was devilish. "Are you saying we should send our regrets and spend the night right here?"

Some of her anxiety eased as she read intent in his casual remark. It seemed that in spite of the glamorous women of Lima, he still desired her. The thought was dangerously pleasant. Pulling herself together, she frowned at him. "Stop teasing me! If you want to know the truth, I'm so nervous I'm almost climbing the walls. I've never been much of a party girl."

"Grace, Grace." He caught her waist and drew her close. His kiss was warm, tender and so sweet she could have wept. She swayed against him as he released her. "Don't be nervous. This party is for my friends and neighbors here in Urubamba. They are good people. You will like them, and they will like you. So come to your party and have a good time."

He offered his arm. Taking it, Grace allowed him to walk her down the hall. She could feel her nervousness ebbing even further. Emilio had a way of calming her fear, just as he had when they were with the horses.

"How is your foot?" he asked, his espresso eyes glancing down at her.

"Fine. Completely healed."

"Then I hope you will dance with me."

Grace stifled a groan. "Something tells me you're a very good dancer."

He laughed. "Not to brag, but yes, I am. It is said that Santana men are born with music in their feet."

"Well, my feet don't have music. And I don't know any of your fancy South American dances. So please don't drag me onto the floor. Not unless you want to see me make a fool of myself."

Stopping, he turned her to face him. "What's wrong with that? If you hide in the corner nothing will happen. But if you get out on the floor and try to dance, people will like you for it."

"And if I fall on my face?"

"Just laugh at yourself. They will laugh with you, and they will love you." For some reason, she got the feeling he was speaking from experience. She found herself wondering what it must have been like for him, growing up in such a prominent family, with his every move under scrutiny. When he fell on his face, the whole country—and sometimes the world—watched to see what he'd do. How difficult that must have been!

She took his arm again. "Where were you when I was a shy, miserable teenager? I could've used that advice."

"Shy? A beauty like you? I don't believe it!"

"I'm still shy. Especially now."

"Don't be." He brushed the back of her hand where it rested on his arm. "And that reminds me, I have a welcoming gift for you. He reached into his pocket and brought out a blue velvet box. "Open it."

Grace's pulse quickened as she took the box and raised

the lid. Inside was an elegantly simple gold cuff bracelet—the real thing, no doubt. Given the price of gold these days, it must have cost a fortune.

"Try it on," Emilio said. "Did I get it right?"

He had. The bracelet was perfect, exactly the sort of design she might have chosen for herself. But how could she accept such an extravagant gift?

She thrust the box toward him. "It's too much. Please, Emilio, take it back."

His eyes twinkled knowingly. "I can't do that. It's already engraved with your name."

"Oh—" She lifted the bracelet out of the box. Her first name was there, engraved in delicate script on the inner surface. Emilio hadn't just grabbed this gift as an afterthought. He'd planned for it and taken extra trouble. Somehow that meant more than the value of the gold.

"Here." Taking the bracelet he slipped it on her left wrist. "See? It was made for you."

He was right. The fit was perfect, the wide, plain style flattering her athletic hand. Grace shook her head. "I don't know what to say," she murmured.

"Thank you is enough." He took her arm again. "Let's go and greet our guests."

Surveying the ballroom, Emilio gave silent thanks to the catering company who'd carried out the arrangements. From the candles and flowers and the lavish buffet to the small live orchestra, everything was suitable. He'd invited about fifty guests—men, women and children—from neighboring estates and farms. They were good-hearted people who, for the most part, could be counted on to make Grace feel welcome.

Her hand trembled on his arm as they walked into the room. She was a vision in the pale dress that set off her golden skin and hair. The gold bracelet on her wrist was the crowning touch. He'd known it was right for her the moment he saw it in a Miraflores jeweler's window.

"Mucho gusto," she said, greeting each guest by name in her limited Spanish as he introduced them. He was proud of her. If she chose to stay, he had no doubt she'd do fine here. And he had to make her stay. He needed a warm, loving woman to help him raise his brother's heir.

And his need for her help was nearly outweighed by his desire for her physically. Remembering the sweetness of her body in bed, Emilio felt his sex stir. He would have to see to it that they had a return engagement soon, maybe tonight.

She glanced up at him as the guests drifted toward the buffet and the dance floor. "This is nice. I didn't expect the children to be invited."

His hand brushed the small of her back. "Everybody comes to parties here. And the children grow up dancing. Look over there."

On the far side of the dance floor, two little girls were doing a wild salsa. A smaller boy joined them, the three shaking their hips and shoulders like dance pros. "In a few years Zac will be dancing like that," he said.

Her smile failed to mask a flicker of despair. Clearly she was still coming to terms with Zac's future.

"What if he turns out to have two left feet?" she asked with a brittle laugh.

"That's not going to happen," Emilio replied. "After all, the boy's a Santana." As the music changed, he seized her waist and swept her onto the open dance floor. "Now, let's have some fun!"

For the first few seconds, Grace froze in his arms. Then she realized that people were watching. Fixing her face in an artificial smile, she tried to follow Emilio's lead. But it was no use. She was stumbling over her own feet.

"I'll skin you alive for this, Emilio Santana!" she hissed through her teeth.

"I can hardly wait." He grinned down at her. "Relax and remember what I told you. You'll do fine."

He pulled her close against him. Now she could feel every inch of his hard male body pressing hers. It was a struggle to keep her mind on the dance. But the tight contact did make it easier to follow his steps. Soon Grace found herself anticipating the weight shifts and hip movements that matched the pulsing beat of the music. She was dancing!

With a triumphant laugh, Emilio spun her to arm's length and flicked her back again. Responding to his subtle cues, she moved in harmony with him, hips swaying with each move. As the music crested he twirled her under his arm and ended the dance with a showy dip. The crowd burst into applause. "You're magnificent," Emilio whispered in her ear.

Flushed and pleased with herself, Grace allowed him to lead her to the refreshment table. Instead of the wine or the ever-present Pisco Sour, she chose a glass of the iced lemonade that had been set out for the children. No alcohol tonight. She felt giddy enough without it.

"Emilio!" The speaker was a woman who must have arrived during the dance. Otherwise Grace would surely have noticed her—a petite Latin beauty with a voluptuous figure and fiery dark eyes. Her ebony hair was pulled into a bun like a flamenco dancer's. On most women the style would have looked matronly, but with her clinging red dress and shoulder-sweeping silver earrings, it was perfect.

"Where have you been, *querido?*" she spoke to Emilio in Spanish, but Grace understood enough to catch her meaning. "I haven't seen you since the funeral. How can you give a party so soon? Aren't you still in mourning?"

"Life goes on, and I mourn in my heart." Emilio replied

in English. "Grace, allow me to present our neighbor, Mercedes Villanueva."

"I'm pleased to meet you." Grace extended her hand and felt the woman's brief, cool clasp.

"Welcome to Peru." Mercedes spoke excellent English. "Did Emilio tell you that I was engaged to his brother? If we'd married, I suppose I would be a widow now. Or perhaps Arturo would not have been driving on that terrible night." She laid a possessive hand on Emilio's arm. The hand remained as she continued. "I am most anxious to see Arturo's son. If things had been different, that little boy might have been mine."

In your dreams, sister. Grace stifled the retort that had sprung to her lips.

"Zac is with the servants now," Emilio said. "But I'll be introducing him soon."

Grace gave him a startled look. No one had mentioned including Zac in the party.

Mercedes turned toward her with a glittering smile. "I saw you dancing. For a beginner you weren't bad. But let me show you a real Latin dance. Come, Emilio." Tightening her clasp on Emilio's arm, she propelled him onto the dance floor. With a nod of her elegant head, she signaled the orchestra to strike up a sensual tango.

As the pair moved to the throbbing beat, other dancers cleared the floor to watch. Even Grace couldn't deny that the two of them were spectacular—Emilio glacial and precise, Mercedes a stalking tigress, her posture blending strength and sexuality. The catlike way she twined herself around him made it clear that, having lost one Santana, she was staking her claim to the other.

He didn't seem to be resisting. The confidence she'd felt in his intentions earlier in the evening faded. Maybe she'd misunderstood. Or maybe, faced with the beautiful Mercedes, he'd simply changed his mind. Fine, she thought to herself, remembering her resolve to avoid getting emotionally invested. Let her have him. But Emilio wasn't all she was after. There was no mistaking the woman's signals. If Mercedes became Emilio's wife, Grace's own days here would be numbered. She'd be smart to keep her bags packed.

But how could she leave Zac, especially to this woman?

The tango ended to rousing applause. Mercedes glided back to the sidelines. She was the most desirable woman in the room, and her smile said she knew it. Feeling like a barnyard goose among bright tropical birds, Grace melted into the crowd. Dancing with Emilio, she'd almost believed she could fit in. Now she knew better. Maybe she should thank Mercedes for bringing her to her senses.

The dancers had spilled back onto the floor. The music seemed louder now, the drums even more compelling. Grace was getting a headache. She glanced around for Emilio but couldn't see him anywhere. Never mind, she would stay a little longer and try to be sociable. When the time was right she could make a discreet exit.

A well-dressed older gentleman whose name Grace had forgotten bowed and invited her to dance. Grace was scrambling for a polite excuse when the music suddenly stopped. The trumpet player blew a two-note fanfare, a signal for attention.

Parting the crowd, Emilio entered from the hallway. Sitting in his arms, dressed in a perfect miniature tuxedo, black tie and shiny black shoes, was Zac.

Zac looked adorable. But he didn't look happy. As the party guests swarmed close, his little face became a thundercloud of confusion and fear. Grace pushed against the packed crowd, struggling to reach him.

Mercedes had come forward to meet the pair. Holding out her arms she took Zac from Emilio. "*Ay,* what a handsome little man!" she cooed in Spanish. "He looks just like his father!"

Zac stared in silence for a moment at the stranger who was holding him. Then he began to howl.

Grace's motherly instincts kicked in. She shoved her way toward him. "Mama!" he sobbed, reaching out with his small arms. "Mama!"

In the next instant she had him. She gathered him close and held him tight. He blubbered against her, smearing her dress with tears as she carried him out into the hall.

Emilio followed her, looking anxious. "Is the boy all right?" he asked.

"He's fine. Just scared half to death, that's all." Clasping Zac protectively, Grace turned on him. "How could you do this—dressing the poor little thing up like an organ-grinder's monkey and taking him into a roomful of strangers? Why didn't you ask me first?"

Emilio looked mortified. "I meant it as a surprise. The secretary I sent to buy the baby monitor came back with the little tuxedo. She said she couldn't resist. The maids put it on him. We thought you'd be pleased."

"Do I look pleased? Does Zac? He's a baby, not some doll you can dress up and show off."

"I'm sorry," Emilio said. "I know I have a lot to learn about children. But I'm trying, Grace. I was trying tonight."

"Next time ask me first." Grace's arms tightened around the hiccupping Zac. "He's worn out. Tell the girls I'm putting him down for the night."

"But you're coming back to the party." It wasn't a question.

"The party's over for me. Go back and enjoy."

Turning away to hide a surge of emotion, Grace fled down the hall. The evening had been a disaster.

As she closed the bedroom door, Pablo's mocking words echoed in her memory like lines from a bad soap opera.

Don *Emilio, he has no heart at all. He cares only for his parties and his women. If you fall in love with him,* querida, *you will be one of many. And in the end you will be sorry. Very sorry.*

Slipping the gold bracelet off her wrist, she dropped it into a dresser drawer.

The party lasted till nearly midnight, when it ended out of deference to the dawning Sabbath. By then the musicians were drooping and most of the children had fallen asleep, to be carried home by their parents.

As host, Emilio was obligated to stay until the last guest had departed. He was bone-weary and concerned about Grace, but to leave would have been unthinkably rude. Only now, having paid generous tips to the musicians and caterers and seen them on the road to the gate, did he find himself alone.

Too tired to sleep, he wandered out to the pool and sank into a chair. The autumn night had taken on a chill. He inhaled the fresh air, letting it clear his head.

By most measures the party had been a success. But it had failed to accomplish what he'd wanted most—making Grace feel welcome.

Mercedes hadn't helped in that respect. Arturo's former fiancée was a stunning woman, but she had a way of viewing every pretty female as a rival. Her sensual tango—which Emilio couldn't have graciously declined—was meant to undermine Grace's confidence. The ploy had worked all too well.

Emilio had known Mercedes Villanueva since childhood. As a girl, she'd been a handful, adventurous and stubborn, but she'd also been kindhearted and affectionate. In the years since, society's grooming and her parents' expectations had whittled away most of the warmth and spontaneity she'd once possessed. He liked her well enough, but he'd understood Arturo's reluctance to go through with the wedding. Mercedes had beauty, style and an impeccable bloodline. But Arturo must have known in his heart that she was turning into a younger version of their mother.

Grace, on the other hand, had never let life, or the countless losses she'd faced, change her intrinsic sweetness. Tender, caring, vulnerable to a fault, a woman like Grace made a man want to stand up and fight her battles—or fight to keep her at his side. He'd never been more certain of that than tonight…as he'd watched her walk away.

Shifting in the chair, Emilio gazed up at the waning moon.

What had possessed him to display Zac in that silly little tuxedo, especially without asking Grace first? He owed her an apology, complete with flowers and dinner at his favorite Cusco restaurant. But it would have to wait until tomorrow. He could only hope she'd forgive his insensitivity. Her forgiveness mattered more than he cared to admit.

Restless now, he rose and prowled along the concrete edge of the pool. He was nearing the far end when he heard unmistakable thumps and moans coming from the pool house. Pablo was up to his tricks again.

Emilio groaned. He should have known the young *cabrón* wouldn't learn from his brother's dismissal. Was he with a local girl or had some female guest left the party for a rendezvous? Never mind, Pablo had been warned. Tomorrow morning there'd be an ugly little scene. The *pícaro* would likely plead his sick mother, though the good woman had been dead for two years. But in the end his fate would be the same as Fermín's.

Hopefully, Pablo would not attempt to cajole him the way Fermín had, claiming that given Emilio's reputation, he should understand the inability to resist a little female temptation. Emilio was *trying;* did no one understand that?

Trying to show that he could change from the man he had been. Trying to show he could be the man that everyone—his employees, Arturo's business associates, Zac and Grace—needed him to be. And the last thing he needed was the likes of Fermín or Pablo hurling constant reminders of his past dissipation in his face.

Arturo, who'd spent much of his time in Lima, had ignored the antics of the two brothers. But Emilio welcomed the chance to replace them with honest family men. The estate was his responsibility now. He wanted workers he could trust.

Responsibility... The word that had once frightened and dismayed him was beginning to sound more natural. The company meetings in Lima had gone surprisingly well, with the board members deferring to his decisions. Could he really do this—take his brother's place as the head of the Santana empire?

Emilio walked back into the house and down the long hallway. Passing Grace's room he paused, imagining her asleep with her nightgown tangled between her lovely thighs. The urge to open her door, steal into her bed and lose himself in that strong, beautiful body was almost more than he could stand.

But what if he were to try the door and find it locked? Or what if she froze with anger when he touched her? Could his male pride take that risk?

Not a chance.

The hand that had reached for the latch dropped to his side. He'd wanted her tonight—and now that he knew he mustn't have her, he wanted her even more. But it wasn't just for sex. He'd had sex with Grace—fabulous, mind-blowing sex. But now, standing outside her door like a moon-eyed idiot, Emilio knew it wasn't enough. He wanted more—more closeness, more intimacy. And true intimacy, as the wise old *curand-*

ero had told him, was a privilege that could only be earned with time and trust.

Steeling his resolve, he turned and continued down the hall. *No strings attached,* he'd told her the first time.

Was he ready to take back those words?

Nine

Emilio had planned to fire Pablo and apologize to Grace the next morning. But plans have a way of changing. He was just drifting into sleep when the phone rang.

The caller from the Lima office was frantic. The Singapore agent who supplied much of South Asia with Santana wines was threatening to back out, leaving a spate of undelivered shipments, unless his contract was renewed with a bigger cut. It was urgent that Emilio come in for a video conference to either negotiate the contract or find a new distributor.

Thirty minutes later he was in his car, bound for the airport in Cusco. He'd barely had time to scribble a note and thrust it under Grace's door. When this current mess was settled, he vowed, his next priority would be a satellite dish upgrade, allowing him to conference from Urubamba. He'd be damned if he was going to waste time shuttling back and forth the way Arturo had.

On the jet he tried to doze. But his thoughts kept wandering to Grace. She'd been magnificent the previous night—so fiercely protective of little Zac. Not that he'd have expected anything less of her. With Grace there were no half measures. Everything she did, she did with the passion of her whole heart.

When had he felt that kind of passion for anything? His jet-setting playboy lifestyle had become a blur of half-remembered parties with women who all looked the same. And he'd stepped into Arturo's job with all the enthusiasm of a swimmer putting a toe into icy water. As for sex, he went about it with a creative skill that satisfied both him and his partners. No complaints—he enjoyed it. But there was a part of himself he'd always seemed to hold back, even with Grace.

The intercom crackled as the pilot spoke. "There's a storm ahead, *Don* Emilio. You'll want to fasten your seat belt."

Emilio straightened his seat and reached around for the belt. The air above the mountains could be brutal in stormy weather. But the pilot was experienced, the Gulfstream jet as sound as any on the market. There was no cause for worry.

He was fastening the buckle when a lightning bolt struck the plane. All in a split second Emilio saw the flash, felt the jolt, heard the deafening boom. The fuselage quivered like a living thing as electricity snaked over its aluminum skin, departing as swiftly as it had come. Then there was nothing but the drone of the plane, the howl of the wind and the slamming of Emilio's heart against his ribs.

"Are you all right, *Don* Emilio?" The pilot's voice crackled over the intercom.

"Yes. How's the plane?" It was a needless question. Modern airplanes like this one were engineered to withstand even the most powerful lightning bolts.

After a pause the answer came. "Everything seems to be

fine. I'll just check…" The words trailed off in a string of curses.

"What is it?" A vague coldness gripped Emilio's chest.

"The left engine's out."

It took a moment for the news to sink in. "From the lightning? But that's not supposed to happen."

There was no reply from the cockpit. The aircraft pitched like a ship on a wild sea as the storm buffeted the wings. Sleet battered the windows. Unbuckling his seat belt Emilio rose, made his way forward to the cockpit and slid into the copilot's seat. At least, from here, he'd be able to see what was happening.

"I tried restarting the cursed thing. No luck." The pilot, Raul Vargas, was a few years older than Emilio with a wife and four children at home in Cusco. "The plane's made to fly on a single engine, but we won't have enough power to climb out of the storm. It's going to be a rough ride."

"What can I do to help?" Emilio asked.

"Just keep a lookout. If I need an extra hand I'll let you know."

"Anything else?"

"Pray."

Emilio hadn't prayed in years. Even if he were to try, he suspected God wouldn't care to listen. Not to him.

For now he peered through the window, where lightning flashes danced among the roiling clouds. Below the plane, fearfully close, the jagged peaks of the Andes jutted like monstrous teeth. Landing was out of the question. The only option was to make it to Lima, or at least to the coast.

If the remaining engine failed or the storm proved too much for the weakened craft, both men would perish. Raul would leave behind a wife, a brood of young children and the aging relatives his income supported. His death would be a tragic loss, felt by all who knew him.

And what would his own death leave behind? Emilio asked himself. Having lived most of his life only for pleasure, he would be mourned by no one. An executor would be found to run the corporate interests and the estate until Zac came of age. The women he'd known would murmur their regrets and move on. The lavish parties would continue without him as they had for the past few weeks already.

Grace, when she thought of him, would remember a presumptuous, arrogant *cabrón* who'd treated her as if he owned her. Zac, his heir, would have no recollection of him at all.

Aside from the wealth that had come through the family, he would leave nothing of value behind. It would be as if he'd never lived.

Thunder cracked across the night-black sky. A savage wind rocked the plane, clawing at the wings as if to rip them from the fuselage. Raul's hands were steady on the controls, but his clenching jaw betrayed the good man's fear. Rigid in his seat, Emilio stared out at the storm. For the first time since his boyhood, his lips moved in silent prayer.

Grace found Emilio's note the next morning. Hastily scrawled on a sheet of white copy paper, its message was brusquely worded.

Urgent business. Flying to Lima. Back as soon as possible.
E.

She read it again. *Urgent business.* That could mean anything. For all she knew, that urgent business could have bedroom eyes and shapely legs. But why should she care? It was no secret that Emilio had plenty of women. The fact that she'd slept with him didn't make her anything special. And she certainly had no right to be jealous.

Was this about last night? She'd been furious, and she'd let him know it. At the time, he'd taken her scolding like a gentleman. But Emilio was first and foremost a Latin male. Being called out by a woman wouldn't set well with him. What if he'd mulled things over and decided he'd had enough of her?

Annoyed with herself, Grace crumpled the note and flung it into the wastebasket. What was wrong with her? She was behaving like an insecure fool. It wasn't as if she really cared for him.

Was it?

Knees giving way, she sank onto the bed and buried her face in her hands. On any list of the stupidest things she could do, falling for Emilio Santana would be close to the top. The man was a tabloid superstar with the morals of a tomcat. He'd bedded glamorous women all over the world. To him, she was nothing more than another notch on his bedpost.

If only she could take Zac and run, get to Cusco and catch a flight to someplace where Emilio couldn't find her. But Grace knew better than to try. Traveling with a small child on a low limit credit card wouldn't get her far. And even if she could fly to the ends of the earth, Emilio would have the resources to track her down.

Besides, would it be fair to Zac to run? This was his family, his blood, his heritage. Didn't she want the best for him? Wasn't it worth some sacrifice on her part to see him well taken care of, settled in a place that tied him to his ancestors and his family legacy?

Leaving, she knew, wasn't an option. All she could do was stay and try to keep her tumultuous emotions under control. When Emilio returned from Lima she would be here. And if

he wanted her, she knew she would be his from the moment
he walked through the door.

She'd just have to hope it wouldn't all end with her broken heart.

By eleven o'clock that morning, Zac was down for his nap
and Grace was enjoying a quiet moment by the pool. She was
slipping into a doze when a shadow fell across her face. She
opened her eyes to find Pablo standing over her.

Startled, she gasped. A smile lit his movie-star handsome
face.

"I am sorry to disturb you, *Doña* Grace. You have a tele-
phone call." He handed her the remote receiver, his gaze sliding down her bare legs.

Ignoring him, she sat up and turned away to take the call.
He remained in place, standing so close that she could smell
the too-sweet cologne on his skin.

"Hello, Grace." The sultry female voice was all too familiar. "It was such a pleasure meeting you last night. I'm
sorry you had to leave with the baby. I was hoping for a
chance to talk."

"Thank you, Mercedes." Grace was cautiously polite. "I'd
have stayed but it was past Zac's bedtime and I didn't want
to leave him."

"Of course. It's your job, after all. But I was hoping Emilio
could spare you for an hour or two. My family owns a hotel
with a fine restaurant here in Urubamba. I'd like to invite
you to lunch for some girl talk. You can bring the little one
along, of course."

Clearly the woman had the wrong impression. "Emilio
had to fly back to Lima," Grace said. "As for the rest, I don't
know what he told you, but I'm not his employee." Even if it
felt that way sometimes. "I'm a guest here."

"Oh." There was a pause on the phone. "But you will let me take you to lunch, won't you?"

"Of course. That's very kind. Zac's napping but he should be awake in an hour."

"Marvelous! I'll pick you up in my car."

Grace ended the call, feeling puzzled. What did Mercedes have in mind, inviting the woman she'd assumed to be a hired nanny to lunch? This had to be more than a friendly chat.

"Can I do anything else for you, *Doña* Grace?" Pablo's breathy purr tickled her ear. "You want a massage? I know how to relax you, make you feel happy all over."

Oh, good grief! Grace shot to her feet, almost knocking him off-balance. "No, I don't need a massage. You can return this phone to where it belongs and then get back to work."

Thrusting the receiver into his hand, she turned and walked away.

Mercedes appeared promptly at one o'clock in her chauffeur-driven German car. By then Grace had fed and bathed Zac and dressed him in a new coverall outfit. There hadn't been much time to make herself presentable, but she'd managed to run a brush through her hair, dab on some lipstick and exchange her shorts for a khaki skirt. Strapping Zac into his car seat, she slung his diaper bag over her shoulder and was out the door.

"I'm so glad you could join me." Mercedes was dressed in a white designer suit with red pumps. Her hair and makeup were flawless. "Oh, and here's our little man, our *hombrecito!*" She chucked Zac under the chin, cooing at him in Spanish as Grace secured the car seat. Zac turned his head, his eyes searching for Grace.

They made small talk on the way to the hotel, a complex of tile-roofed buildings set in a lush landscape of trees and flowers. The restaurant overlooked a lily pond where koi swam in lazy circles.

The waiter led them to a table near the window and brought a high chair for Zac. The exchange of pleasantries continued until, over a salad of crisp greens and fruits, Mercedes finally broached the real business at hand.

"Arturo's son seems very attached to you." She glanced at Zac, who was mouthing a mango slice Grace had given him.

"That's to be expected," Grace said. "I've raised him from birth."

"Yes, I know about his mother. Arturo told me."

Grace's defenses prickled a warning. "Then you know that Arturo gave me permission to adopt him."

"He did—at my suggestion. We were planning to marry. I wanted to protect the family assets for our future children."

"So the stipulation that Zac have no claim on the Santana estate was *your* idea."

"It seemed prudent at the time." Mercedes speared a strawberry and raised it to her crimson lips. "But Arturo's death changed everything. Emilio took over. He could have claimed the entire estate for himself, but he insisted on bringing the boy home to raise as Arturo's heir—and possibly his own, since he's never shown much interest in starting a family."

Grace glanced at Zac, who was making a sticky mess of the mango slice. Something was going on here, and it all had to do with Zac. She hoped she was about to find out what it was.

"You must have been devastated when Emilio showed up to claim the child," Mercedes said.

"*Devastated* isn't the word for it. That's why I agreed to come here as well, because I couldn't bear to be parted from Zac."

Mercedes nodded. "You're everything a mother should be. That's why I have a proposition to make. How would you like to get your little boy back—for keeps this time?"

The salad fork dropped from Grace's fingers and clattered onto the tablecloth. Mercedes smiled.

"Don't look so startled. I have the means to fly you and Zac out of Peru and settle you anyplace you want to go. My offer would include enough money for a new start—say, half a million U.S. dollars. I could even arrange for a legal adoption. Since everything would be done privately, no one, including Emilio, should be able to trace you. It would be like your…what do you call it? Your witness protection program."

Grace recovered her voice. "But why would you do this? What's in it for you?"

No sooner had she asked the question than the answer fell into place. With Zac out of the way, Emilio would be duty-bound to marry and father an heir. And who would make a more suitable wife than his late brother's beautiful, wealthy fiancée?

"I'm not a bad person, Grace," Mercedes said. "I cared for Arturo and I want the best for his son. The best, I believe, is a life with you as his mother."

"And what about Emilio? Do you love him?"

"Emilio and I have been friends since we were children. I understand him, and I can give him what he needs. How many other women can claim that—including you?"

There was a beat of tense silence. Zac chose that moment to fling a handful of smashed mango toward Mercedes. The gooey mess struck the lapel of her spotless white jacket and clung there. Zac giggled with delight as the stain spread, soaking into the costly raw silk.

The shock that flashed across Mercedes's face was swiftly replaced with an icy composure. Dipping a napkin into her water glass, she dabbed off the worst of the mango, although enough remained to ruin her elegant suit.

Mortified, Grace found her voice. "I'm so sorry! I hope you'll at least let me pay for the damage."

Mercedes managed a cold smile. "Don't worry about it, *querida*. With children, these things happen. But never mind. We were discussing my offer. If you're smart, you'll accept it."

Grace began cleaning Zac with a wipe from the diaper bag. "Generous as it is, Mercedes, I could never take your money. Right now, what I need is to take this little hooligan out of here before he does something worse. Would you mind taking us home?"

"Of course not." Mercedes rose, her carmine lips still fixed in a smile. "But don't say no just yet. My offer remains open. A foreign visa would take a little time to arrange, but if you choose to settle in the U.S. you could be gone before Emilio gets back from Lima. I'll give you my private number. Think about it and let me know if you change your mind."

Grace was silent on the short drive home but her emotions were in turmoil. She'd declined Mercedes's help out of pride. But wasn't this what she'd wanted, to take Zac and flee out of Emilio's reach forever? To raise Cassidy's child as her own and rescue her heart from the impossibly charming rake who seemed on the verge of stealing it?

Why remain here in the shadow of other people's lives, nurturing a child who could never be hers and maybe even falling for a man who would never marry her? It was so tempting to run away and leave all those problems behind. But what new problems would running create? She needed time to think, to be sure.

The car passed through the gate and pulled up to the house. As the driver came around to help with Zac's car seat, Mercedes laid a manicured hand on Grace's arm. "Take as long as you need to decide. Either way, promise you won't tell Emilio about my offer. If you do, I'll deny everything."

"I won't tell him." The promise came easily. Whether she left or stayed, Grace had no wish to make a dangerous enemy.

Back in her room, she changed into slacks and the sneakers she'd bought and dropped Zac off in the kitchen with the maids. What she needed was a long, solitary walk. Striking out across the patio, she skirted the pool and headed across the lawn. She was nearing the paddock when a thought struck her.

She'd ridden once with Emilio and managed all right until the horse bolted. Was she strong enough to do it on her own?

What would she miss if she never rode again in her life?

Steeling her nerves, she strode toward the stable. The groom—not Pablo's handsome younger brother but a middle-aged man with a gentle face—was outside filling a water bucket.

"May I help you *señorita?*" he asked in halting English.

"Yes, thank you. I'd like to ride Manso. Can you help me saddle him?"

"Of course." His smile revealed a missing front tooth. "*Don* Emilio said you might come. He told me to help you. I am Juan, *a su servicio.*"

So Emilio had thought she might want to ride again. Had it been a lucky guess, or did he understand her better than she'd realized?

She waited as Juan led the bridled gelding out of the stable. She stood by the graceful head, stroking and talking to the horse as the saddle was strapped into place. "Neither of us had a great time before, did we, old boy? But this time will be better, Manso. Wait and see."

Her nerves crawled as she waved away Juan's proffered hand, thrust her left foot into the stirrup and swung into the saddle. Sensing her unease, the horse snorted and danced. Grace stroked the warm, satiny neck, her heart pounding.

"Will you be all right, *señorita?*" Juan asked.

She nodded, her lips pressed into a tight line.

Juan laid a calming hand on the gelding's shoulder. "Keep

to the trails. If you get lost, give him his head. He knows the way home."

"I'll remember that. *Gracias,* Juan." She nudged Manso to a walk and felt his easy gait flowing beneath her. Little by little, her clenched muscles began to relax.

The day was warm and sunny, the trees alive with bird-calls. Grace took the path she'd ridden with Emilio, through the trees and winding up into the foothills. Something tight-ened around her heart as she passed the spot where he'd held her in his arms, calmed her fears; the spot where they'd kissed for the first time. How proud he'd be if he could see her, knowing he'd inspired her to face her fear. Wherever life took her, she would have the memory of that day—and gratitude for the courage he'd awakened in her.

A white butterfly drifted across her vision and vanished in a haze of sunlight. It was so beautiful here. Despite her-self, Grace had grown attached to this land—and to the peo-ple in it. She brushed away a tear. Could she take Zac and leave without a word, knowing how betrayed Emilio would feel? Could she start a new life, knowing she would never see him again?

If she stayed, she'd end up with nothing but loneliness and heartache. Mercedes's offer could be her salvation—her one chance of keeping Zac. A cousin of her mother's lived on a Wyoming ranch. Surely they'd take her in for a week or two, until she decided where to settle. With money, anything was possible—and she would have money. All she had to do was go back to the house and pick up the phone.

But would it be honest? Would it be fair to Emilio? Could she live the rest of her life knowing what she'd done to him?

And what about Zac's future? Could she deprive him of his rightful heritage for the sake of her own selfish needs? Would he grow up to resent the choice she'd made for him?

Just one thing was certain. She needed more time to reach

a decision. That would mean more time with Emilio and more risk to her heart. But she had to be sure. This was the only way.

More troubled than ever, she turned the horse and rode back toward the stable.

Ten

Emilio roused from a doze as the car pulled up to the darkened house. His management of the Asian crisis had gone well, with the demanding agent replaced by a new partner. But after the harrowing flight to Lima, followed by three hectic days of living on coffee, he was burned out. He was ready for some rest and renewal at home.

And now he *was* home. For the past decade the old family estate had been little more than a stopping place between trips and parties, or a venue to host parties of his own. Now it had become *home,* a place that called to him when he was away and embraced his return with a feeling of welcome.

What had changed for him here? He knew the answer to that question. Now he needed to make sure Grace knew it, too. He'd tried calling her once from Lima, but had changed his mind and hung up after the second ring, What he wanted to say should be said face-to-face.

"Should I take your bag to your room, *Don* Emilio?" His

driver had opened the car door and was waiting with the suitcase at his feet.

Emilio stifled a yawn. "I'll take it, Francisco. Put the car away and get some sleep."

As the vehicle disappeared around the side of the house, Emilio crossed the portico and unlocked the front door. He could have stayed in Lima and flown home in the morning. But the weather had been clear and he'd been anxious to leave the city. He'd been there long enough.

Only his driver, who'd received the last-minute call, had known he was on his way home. Now it was after midnight. The household was asleep, which was just as well. All he wanted was to stumble inside and fall into bed.

But whose bed? The thought of stealing into Grace's room, crawling between the sheets and spooning her sweet body against his was so tempting it made him ache. But they hadn't parted on the best of terms. He couldn't assume he'd be welcome. Wisdom dictated that he wait until tomorrow, after they'd settled a few things.

Crossing to the back hallway, he glimpsed a pale, moving shape through the glass doors that opened on to the patio. Someone was out there.

Leaving his suitcase in the hall he walked to the patio door. Surprisingly, the latch was unlocked. Was it an oversight or had someone stolen out of the house, planning to return?

On silent feet, he stepped outside. Moonlight flooded the patio, casting the ferns into a filigree of lacy shadow. A light breeze carried the scent of jasmine from the vine that hung over the roof.

Was he alone? No, he saw her now, standing half in shadow with her back toward him. It was Grace.

What was she doing out here at this hour? Waiting for something? For someone? As the possibility struck him, a blast of possessive rage flared in Emilio's tired mind. If Pablo so much as laid a hand on her, he wasn't just going to fire the *malcriado*. He was going to beat him into the ground.

But what was he thinking? This was Grace—his smart, sensible Grace. She'd know better than to succumb to a horny young *cabrón* like Pablo. And she wasn't dressed for a rendezvous. Her robe was flung carelessly over her rumpled nightgown. Her hair was tangled from sleep—or maybe from trying to sleep. In one hand she held an object he recognized as the receiver for her baby monitor.

He watched as she placed the monitor on a side table and sank into a chair. Hunching her shoulders, she buried her face in her hands.

Crossing the patio, Emilio touched her shoulder. She glanced up with startled eyes. "I'm here, Grace," he said. "Tell me what's wrong."

If only she dared tell him. Since refusing Mercedes's offer, Grace had been through agonies of indecision. Two different times she'd picked up the phone, dialed the number Mercedes had given her, and then disconnected the call before the phone could ring. Now, looking up into Emilio's worried face, she couldn't help wondering what he would have done if he'd returned to find her gone.

"What is it?" he asked, pulling up a chair and sitting to face her.

"Couldn't sleep." At least that much was true.

"You're shivering. Are you cold?"

She shook her head, but he stripped off his light jacket and laid it around her shoulders. She nestled into it, warmed by the heat his body had left. "How was Lima?" she asked, changing the subject before he could question her further.

"Crazy. I barely slept. Couldn't wait to get home. You got my note, didn't you?"

"What there was of it."

"I was in a rush." He gave her a brief explanation of the problem with the shipping agent. "That's the trouble with doing business in Asia. You have to show up at all hours to conference with them."

"But you worked it out?"

"Yes, everything's fine." He settled back in the chair. Moonlight deepened the shadows beneath his eyes. He looked so tired. Grace resisted the urge to lean forward and brush the rumpled curls back from his forehead. She was struggling with the most painful decision of her life. Reaching out to him would only deepen the conflict.

"I meant to call, but it didn't happen," he said.

"I wasn't expecting you to. I realized you'd have a lot on your mind."

"It wasn't that. The truth is, you and Zac were on my mind a great deal. But what I have to say, I didn't want to say on the phone."

Grace's pulse broke into a gallop. "I'm here now," she said. "And I'm listening."

In the silence that followed, Grace could hear the chirr of crickets in the undergrowth and the splash of water in the fountain. An eternity seemed to pass before he spoke.

"We had a rough trip into Lima. Worse than rough. We ran into a storm over the mountains, got hit by lightning, lost an engine…" He paused, raking a hand through his hair. "I owe my life to Raul's skill as a pilot. But for the last thirty minutes of the flight, I wasn't sure we were going to make it. A man can have some serious thoughts when he thinks he's facing the end."

He fell silent. Grace willed herself to keep still and wait for him to go on. Was she about to hear something that would make a difference? Would it ease her decision or make it even harder?

"I hardly knew my father," he said. "Between his work and his women, he didn't have much time for his family. When he died I was in my late teens and already drifting away from family obligations. I can't say I shed many tears.

"Arturo had been groomed to succeed him, and he took his responsibilities to heart. My brother was the hardest worker I've ever known. He left the Santana holdings in fine shape, but aside from Zac he left no family. Looking back, if I'd stayed around and given him some help, he might have had more of a life outside work. I blame myself for that."

"What about Mercedes?" Grace couldn't resist asking.

"Marriage would have been a practical arrangement for them both. At least she would have given him children. But the wedding got pushed back several times because he kept having work conflicts with the chosen dates for the wedding and honeymoon. He did intend to marry her and fulfill his duty to the family, but he was far from an eager groom. As far as I know, the only woman he ever loved was Cassidy."

"I'm sorry. That's terribly sad."

"Yes, it is." His fingertips skimmed the back of her hand, then withdrew. "But the most pathetic figure of all is the one you see in front of you. *The Peruvian Playboy.*" He shook his head. "In all my life, Grace, I haven't accomplished one damned thing of worth."

"How can you say that?" The protest sprang to her lips.

"Listen to me. While that plane was limping along on one engine in a raging storm, I realized that if I died, my life would have no more consequence than putting my hand in a river and taking it out again. I promised myself then and there that if I lived through the night, things were going to change."

He rose, wired and restless with plans yet to be carried out. "I want to run the family business the way Arturo would have run it, only better, with more benefits for the workers— better pay, better working conditions, more security. Another layer of management, too, so that tasks and responsibilities can be delegated. I intend to see to it that the work is done and done well, but I won't let it consume my life the way Arturo did. And I want to do something for the poor families here in Urubamba—a school for the village, maybe a clinic. I've got the money. Why not put it to use?"

He paused, aware perhaps, that he was rambling. "Sorry, I must sound like a crazy man. It'll all make more sense in the morning, but there's one more thing you need to know. I want to be a real father to Zac—to spend time with him, have fun with him and teach him what's important. If I can do it right, he won't grow up to be a workaholic like his father or a wastrel like me. But for that, I'm going to need you, Grace. I'm going to need you with me every step of the way."

Grace stared up at him. She knew better than to think the man had just proposed marriage. His words sounded more like an offer of permanent employment. But hearing them, she knew she wouldn't be taking Mercedes's offer. It was Zac's future that mattered. The best and brightest version of that future appeared to be right here.

And Emilio was here, too. Seeing him like this, passionate and idealistic, committing his whole heart to being a better man, she could no longer deny the truth. She loved him. And if he needed her on this journey to the future he planned, then she'd be there beside him—right up until the moment when he didn't need her any more.

"Promise me you'll stay, Grace," he said. "Zac needs you. *I* need you."

He opened his arms. Rising, she walked into them and laid her head against his chest. As he held her, she felt the scattered pieces of her world fall into place. If only this could be for always. But that was asking too much of fate. She and Emilio were different people with complicated lives. Tomorrow, the next day or the next year, something was bound to change. She would have to be prepared for that.

"I want to stay," she whispered. "But only a fool would promise to stay forever. Let's just say that I'll stay for now. Tomorrow will have to take care of itself. All right?"

"All right." His lips brushed her tangled hair. "I'll just have to keep you happy enough to stick around."

If only it were that simple. She pressed her face into his shirt, filling her senses with the manly aroma of his body. Emilio was kind, fair and generous. As long as she stayed he would treat her well. And while the chemistry between them remained strong, he would probably even sleep with her. But she couldn't ask him for the one thing she wanted.

She couldn't demand that he love her.

His hand shifted to raise her chin for a kiss. But before their lips could meet, a plaintive wail rose from the baby monitor.

"Maaaa-maaaa!"

He released her, his mouth quirking in a smile. "That sounds like duty calling. Go on. I'll see you in the morning."

Picking up the baby monitor, Grace turned to go, then stopped herself. "Oh, no, you don't," she said, seizing his hand. "You wanted to be a father. So put your money where your mouth is and come with me."

"Grace, I'm worn out. I need sleep."

"Too bad. Welcome to fatherhood."

Exhausted but amused, Emilio allowed himself to be dragged into the house and down the hall toward Grace's bedroom. He was stronger than she was. He could have put his foot down and ordered her to let him go. But he was intrigued by Grace's behavior. How far was she going to take this?

By the time they reached the bedroom, the cries from the

baby monitor had risen to outraged howls. Grace rushed into the nursery, pulling Emilio behind her. Zac was standing up in his crib, flinging himself against the rail as he gave voice to his frustration. Letting go of Emilio's hand, Grace walked to the crib and lifted the baby in her arms. The cries stopped as if someone had flipped a switch. The night-light illuminated a small, tear-streaked face.

"Is he all right?" Emilio asked.

"He's fine. Just scared when he woke up and nobody was here." Grace cradled Zac against her shoulder. "Before long he'll be big enough to climb out of the crib and go adventuring. Then we'll really have to watch him."

We. Emilio hadn't missed her meaning. When he'd said he wanted to be a father to Zac, he'd meant it. But was he up for the challenge he had taken on?

"He's wet," she said. "Would you mind holding him while I get a diaper and some clean jammies?" Without waiting for an answer she thrust the baby into Emilio's arms.

Emilio had held Zac before so that, at least, was nothing new. The child eyed him curiously, then reached up to touch the stubble on his chin. The whiskery, sandpaper feel triggered a startled look, then a gap-toothed grin. "Oh, so you like that, do you?" Emilio held one chubby little hand and brushed it along his jaw. Zac giggled with delight. Arturo's son was already a charmer.

"See? You're a natural with babies." Grace took Zac and laid him on a padded table. "Do you want to try changing him, or would you rather observe?"

"Silly question. Go ahead." Emilio stood at the foot of the table and watched as her expert hands removed the damp pajamas and unfastened the tabs on the disposable diaper. How could he explain to her that this wasn't part of the bargain? Peruvian fathers, even good ones, didn't change diapers.

Tossing the wet diaper into a covered bin, she unfolded a

clean one, laid it underneath Zac's rosy bottom and reached for a lubricated wipe. Emilio made a mental note to order a crate of fresh supplies for this operation.

"Back in the old days—" he started to say. But his words were interrupted by a warm liquid stream dousing the front of his shirt. Zac was spouting like a fountain—and giggling like a little imp!

"Oh, no!" Grace stared at Emilio's shocked face, biting back laughter.

"I'd swear he did that on purpose!" Emilio muttered, glancing around for a towel. "Look at that grin!"

"Would it help if I told you he only pees on people he likes?" Losing control, Grace burst into giggles. "I'm sorry... the look on your face...it's priceless!"

"At least the kid's got a good aim," Emilio grumbled, trying to see some humor in the situation. "Now excuse me while I clean myself up."

Leaving the nursery, he made his way to the bathroom attached to Grace's room and turned on the light. The face that looked back at him from the mirror-tiled wall was gaunt, unshaven and red-eyed with weariness. But, inexplicably, he was smiling. There was something about a baby...

He felt as if he'd just been baptized into a strange new order called fatherhood.

His shirt was hopelessly soaked. Unbuttoning it, he laid it over the side of the laundry bin. His singlet had fared better but it was damp and smelled of wet baby. He stripped that off as well, and wiped down his chest and shoulders with a fresh washcloth. What he really needed was a shower. But he was too weary for that. He would say good-night to Grace, get his suitcase from the hall and stumble off to bed.

When he returned to the darkened bedroom, Grace was

still in the nursery with Zac. The night-light glowed faintly through the half-open doorway. Not wanting to disturb the baby, but too tired to wait, he decided on a stealthy exit.

He'd started for the hall door when a sound reached his ears. He stood transfixed, listening. Grace was singing a lullaby.

Her untrained voice was soft and warm, caressing each note of the gentle song. The melody was unfamiliar but the words painted images of enchantment—moonlight shining, birds closing their eyes, angels watching through the night...

Zac must have been slow falling asleep because the song went on and on, weaving a hypnotic spell. The urge to sleep weighted Emilio's eyelids. He knew he should go to his room but with Grace's lullaby flowing through him like clear water, he couldn't bring himself to leave.

Bone weary, he sank onto the edge of the bed, shed his shoes and socks, and stretched out on the sheet. He would lie here a few moments, resting and waiting for Grace to finish her song. Then he would bid her good-night and wander back to his own bed.

Lulled by her voice, he closed his eyes.

With a sigh of relief, Grace lowered Zac into the crib and covered him with his favorite blue blanket. Wide-awake after Emilio's visit, he'd taken his time falling back to sleep. But her lullaby had finally done the trick. Maybe now she could get some rest.

Had she gone too far, pushing Emilio into fatherhood? He hadn't looked amused when Zac squirted him. And he hadn't returned to the nursery after leaving to clean up. Maybe she shouldn't have laughed at him. Latin men did seem to place a high value on their dignity.

Stealing away from the crib she crept out the door and

closed it behind her. The bedroom was dark, but slanting rays of moonlight revealed a half-clad form on the bed. Sprawled like a child, Emilio lay fast asleep on the bottom sheet.

When she spoke his name, the only response was a muffled snore. Clearly he was there to stay—and in no frame of mind for seduction. So why not make him comfortable? Bending over him, Grace unfastened his trousers and eased them off his legs, leaving him clad in nothing but his wristwatch and his black silk briefs.

Through all this, Emilio scarcely moved except for the rise and fall of his chest. He was beautiful in sleep, she thought, looking down at him. His damp hair curled over his forehead, above straight black brows and lashes that lay like inky smudges against his tanned cheeks. His body was an athlete's, lean, muscular and superbly toned, with a dusky triangle of dark hair shading his chest. Beneath the thin layer of knit silk, his sex lay at rest—impressive even in that condition. It seemed a shame to cover him, Grace mused, but she pulled up the covers and tucked them around his slumbering body.

She hadn't had much sleep herself. Tossing her robe on a chair, she slipped into bed beside him. His sleep-warmed body took up most of the double mattress. Only by snuggling close to his side could Grace find enough room. Her arm stole across his chest, binding him to her. The sensation was bittersweet. She savored it for what it was, aware that despite their new accord, nights like this, with Emilio sleeping in her arms, would be precious and few.

She would gladly spend every night of her life in this man's bed. But she knew better. Much as she loved Emilio, she could never be the wife he needed.

She was American. She was unsophisticated. She lacked

the family connections or social graces that a Santana lady was supposed to possess.

And worst of all, she was damaged goods, with a broken body that could never give him a family.

Eleven

In Emilio's dream he was standing at the entrance to the Santana family crypt in Cusco. He carried four red roses—one for each departed member of his family. The freshly cut flowers were flawless but the thorns on the stems sliced like razors into his flesh. His blood spattered the stone floor as he walked into the crypt and stopped before the niche that held his father's casket.

As he laid one rose on the open ledge, he heard his father's sharp voice, so plain and clear that he shuddered in his sleep. *What right do you have to come here? Your brother did his duty and carried on after me. But you—what have you done except play? Go. Don't come back until you're worthy.*

Shaken, Emilio moved to his mother's resting place. Choosing the most beautiful rose he laid it beside her framed photograph and heard her plaintive whisper.

You were the child I loved best, Emilio. The gentlest and most caring. Where did you go when things went bad for me? Why weren't you there when I needed you?

Fleeing her bitter words, Emilio chose the smallest rose for Roberto, his firstborn brother who'd died in childhood. Emilio had been little more than a baby at the time. But he could still recall his brother's swollen belly and the sad little coffin that held him like a misshapen doll.

Don't forget me, Emilio. The voice in his ear was not a child's, yet not a man's. *I lived, and it wasn't for nothing. Think, remember and learn...*

Unable to bear any more, Emilio moved on. One rose remained. He carried it to the niche where Arturo's remains rested. His was the one voice Emilio wanted to hear. Would Arturo offer some guidance, or even a word of blessing? Emilio laid the rose in its proper place and waited.

Nothing.

"Arturo." He pleaded. "Speak to me."

But no answer came. The crypt was as silent as death.

Emilio burst from the dream like a swimmer coming up for air. For a moment he lay still, lost in confusion. Then he remembered coming home late, being in Grace's bedroom and drifting off to her lullaby.

The room was dark, the morning birds still silent. In the stillness he could hear Grace's whispery breath. She was curled on her side, her hair tickling his bare shoulder, her adorable bum pillowing his hip.

When was the last time he'd slept with a woman without having sex first? A smile teased Emilio's lips. Never mind the question. Lying next to Grace in the quiet dawn, he felt wrapped in peace—a peace he craved after the vividly wrenching dream.

Lying still so as not to disturb her, he went through the dream in his mind. The old *curandero* had spoken to him about dreams. Emilio could still picture the ancient figure sitting cross-legged in the firelight, wrapped in his faded

poncho, his sparse hair covered by the new *chullo* cap Emilio
had brought as a gift, along with a box of the chocolates Dolores had mentioned he loved.

Dreams should never be dismissed, he'd told Emilio.
Dreams about departed family were of special gravity. They
carried messages that should be heeded.

What would the old man make of Emilio's dream?

Emilio wasn't superstitious, but now he tried to open his
mind to the dream's meaning. The voices of his father and
mother had likely risen from his own guilt. He *had* been a
disappointing son. Not that they'd have won any prizes as
parents. But he might have made more effort to please them,
or at least to understand them.

Arturo's silence was a message in itself. Emilio hadn't listened to his brother in life. Why should he listen now? He was
on his own. There was nothing more for his brother to say.

Only Roberto's words remained a mystery. Emilio had
barely known his sickly brother and had never heard him
speak in life. What could he learn from an impaired child
who'd died before he was old enough to go to school?

Grace stirred in her sleep, sliding against his thigh. The
contact sent a jolt of awareness through Emilio's body. Why
was he muddling about dreams when there was a warm,
beautiful, very real woman next to him in the bed?

Grace had been tired last night. Emilio knew she needed
her rest. But he couldn't resist rolling onto his side and spooning against her. As he fitted his body to hers, she sighed and
nestled her rump into the hollow of his hips. The fit was perfect, the feeling pure bliss. Emilio felt the tension and worry
easing out of him. He'd never known that just holding someone could feel so good.

He closed his eyes and willed himself to go back to sleep.
But one part of his body was wide-awake. Where her bot-

tom rested against his black silk briefs, his sex had sprung to a quivering, rock-hard erection.

Savoring the torment, he pulled her close, rubbing against her just enough to heighten the sensation. A groan rumbled in his throat. Never in his life had he wanted more to be inside a woman, thrusting deep into that wet, silken honey. That he refrained to let her get the rest she needed was something new and unfamiliar.

Her skin smelled of the handmade goats' milk soap Dolores bought for the guest rooms. The flowery scent was familiar, but Grace's own chemistry added a note of pure sensuality. The pheromone-like aroma was driving him wild. Unable to resist, he nuzzled the nape of her neck, drinking her into his senses. Mussed and sound asleep, she was the sexiest woman he'd ever encountered in his life.

With a little moan she stirred in his arms. Then, as if it were the most natural thing in the world, she turned to face him on the pillow. Her hazel eyes opened. She smiled, deepening the dimple at the corner of her mouth.

How long had the minx been awake?

A good morning whisper formed in Emilio's throat, but before he could speak she laid a silencing finger against his lips. Her gaze twinkled with subtle mischief as she captured his hand and guided it down to the nest of curls between her open thighs.

She was dripping moisture.

With a muttered oath, he yanked down his briefs, found a condom in the drawer, rolled on top of her and thrust home. As soon as he entered her she came, clenching around his shaft in a chain of spasms that rocked him to the core. No finesse, no games—she was his woman and this was where he belonged, filling her urgent need with his own.

Her legs wrapped his hips, satiny thighs cradling him close as he kissed her throat, her eyelids, her soft, sleepy

mouth. Such a feeling of welcome. It was as if he'd been
wandering all his life and finally come home. He loved the
scent of her, the taste of her, the way her breasts molded to
his chest as her hands clasped his straining buttocks, pulling
each thrust deep inside her. Her little whimpers mounted as
she crested toward another climax. Feeling its surge, he un
leashed his own and burst with her in a shuddering mingle
of bodies and souls.

She gazed up at him as they drifted back to earth like
the glowing fragments of spent fireworks. Her lips moved
whispering tender, half-understood words. Lying there be
neath him, their bodies still joined, she was the most beau
tiful thing he'd ever known.

As Emilio kissed her and eased back onto his own pillow
he remembered the counsel of the wise old *curandero*—that
real intimacy was a privilege to be earned with time and trust

It might be too soon, but something told him he'd jus
achieved real intimacy…and made love.

When he woke again to early daylight Grace was gone
The place where she'd slept beside him was empty, the shee
cool. Without her in it the bed felt wide and lonely.

Emilio was about to get up and find her when the nurs
ery door swung open. Grace stepped into the bedroom with
Zac in her arms. Washed, combed and dressed in one of the
little romper suits she favored, Zac looked ready for the day

Grace had clearly put his needs ahead of her own. He
robe was hastily knotted, her hair tousled, her face bare o
makeup; but she still managed to look meltingly sexy.

"Good morning." She gave him a shy smile, as if unsure
of what to say to him after last night. "Did you sleep well?"

Her question sounded so innocent that he had to chuckle
"I'd say I slept about as well as you did."

Was she blushing? Whatever was going on, she looked

delicious enough to make him want her all over again. If she hadn't been holding the baby he'd have been tempted to lure her back into bed for some serious play between those long, lovely legs. Heaven save him, would he ever get enough of this woman?

"I brought your suitcase in from the hall." She glanced down to where Emilio's bag sat at the foot of the bed. "I thought you might want to freshen up before you venture out. I can wait my turn in the bathroom."

"Go ahead. For now, I'm happy where I am." Emilio pushed himself to a semi-reclining position and leaned back into the pillows, enjoying the view.

"In that case, would you mind watching Zac while I shower? He likes to play on the bed. I promise I won't be long. Is that all right?"

"That depends. Is he safely diapered?"

The dimple deepened in her cheek. "Guaranteed." She lowered the baby onto the foot of the bed. "He knows enough not to fall. Just keep him out of trouble."

She vanished into the bathroom, closing the door. Seconds later Emilio heard the sound of the shower. Willing his thoughts away from visions of soap bubbles sliding over Grace's naked body, he fixed his attention on his nephew.

Sitting where Grace had left him, Zac gazed at Emilio in fascination. "What are you looking at, you little rascal?" Emilio muttered. "You've seen me before. Nothing new here."

But something was different. It took a moment's puzzling before Emilio realized what it was. It appeared the boy had never seen a man without clothes. He was staring at the hair on Emilio's chest.

"So you want to check your old uncle out, do you? Come here, then." Emilio motioned Zac closer. Curiosity winning over caution, the youngster crawled forward until he was crouched on Emilio's knees. One small hand reached out and brushed Emilio's chest. "See, it's just hair." Emilio touched the boy's head. "Hair."

"Ha...ar." Zac mimicked. Then, before Emilio could recover from his surprise, the tot seized a fistful of his chest hair and gave it an experimental yank. Emilio winced, biting back a curse. Zac giggled. His laugh sounded a bit like Cassidy's—and Cassidy had possessed a mischievous streak, as well. The boy was very much his mother's child. Maybe more of Arturo's traits would emerge as he grew up.

"No hair pulling." Emilio lifted the little scamp and set him back on the foot of the bed. In the bathroom, the sound of Grace's shower had stopped. Zac glanced toward the bathroom door. "Mama?"

"Not yet." Scrambling for a distraction, Emilio tossed a loose end of the blanket over Zac's head. "Where's Zac?" he asked in mock consternation. "I don't see him anywhere!"

Zac seemed to know this game. He lifted the edge of the blanket and peeked out, grinning. Emilio covered him again and repeated the game. Each time he was "found" Zac grew more delighted, squealing with laughter.

"See? I said you were a natural." Wrapped in a towel, Grace was standing in the open doorway of the bathroom, her hair damp, her face smiling. "I've never seen Zac take to anybody the way he takes to you."

"Mama!" Game forgotten, Zac scooted toward the edge of the bed.

"Maybe so, but I can see I'm not at the top of his list." Emilio reached out to keep Zac in place. "I think he wants to get down. Does he need help?"

"A little. Just take his arms."

Emilio lowered Zac feet first off the side of the bed. Zac stood for a moment, one hand clasping the sheet. Then he turned and took a first tottering step toward Grace.

"Oh!" Grace's eyes lit with wonder. She knelt, coaxing him toward her. "Come on, Zac. Come to me."

Zac took one more wobbly step, then another before toppling forward into Grace's arms. "You did it, big boy! You walked! I'm so proud of you!" Grace hugged him, beside herself with excitement.

Watching the two of them, Emilio felt an unaccustomed yearning—a desire to take these two joyful people and make them his own. His *family*. The word triggered an ache in his throat. Not the dismal sort of family he'd grown up in, but a close-knit family with two parents who loved each other and raised their child together.

It was too soon, the voice of caution whispered. He needed more time with Grace and Zac, time to think things over and be sure. The last thing he wanted was a marriage like his parents'. When and if he wed, he intended to be a faithful husband. Was he ready yet to settle down and do that after the life he'd led? He had to be certain.

Grace had donned her robe and was encouraging Zac to take more steps on his own. While they were occupied, Emilio pulled on his trousers and slipped into his shirt. He would bathe and put on clean clothes in his own room. Then he needed to catch up on some paperwork—and fire that scapegrace, Pablo.

"You're leaving us?" Grace glanced up at him.

"I'll be back in time to help celebrate our boy's first steps. How about a nice lunch in town for the three of us?"

"Thanks, but we'll pass for now. I'm guessing you've never eaten in public with an eleven-month-old. Zac can be a little pill when he wants to be. And even if he's on good behavior, he won't know what the fuss is about. Just being able to walk will be celebration enough for him."

"Then maybe later, just you and me." Emilio liked the

idea of a romantic date. He craved some time alone with her, and not just in bed.

"I have a different suggestion." Her eyes twinkled with mystery. "If you're free after lunch, why not meet me at the stables for a ride?"

"A ride?" Emilio remembered Grace's terror of horses. Now here she was, talking about it as if it were nothing. "But—"

A smile softened her face. "No buts. If you show up, I just might have a surprise for you. Run along, now. I'll see you later."

Her gentle laugh trailed him out the door. Had she faced her fear and taken up riding again? It couldn't have been easy for her, but it appeared she'd done exactly that. She was as courageous as she was beautiful.

As Emilio strode down the hall with his suitcase, one thought firmed in his mind. If ever a woman deserved to be loved, it was Grace Chandler. Was he capable of giving her the kind of love she needed—a lifetime of unselfish devotion?

Before he gave her his promise he would have to know for sure. Anything less would be cruel.

Grace kept her composure until the door had clicked shut behind Emilio. Only then did she let her smile slip and disappointment flood in. For a moment, she'd been lulled into thinking of them as a family unit—man, woman and child. But he had walked away so easily.

She'd been moved by Emilio's resolve to be a good father to Zac. And she'd been swept away by his ardent lovemaking. But that didn't mean he loved her. And even if he did, or thought he did, who could say that those feelings would last? Temporary desire wouldn't make them right for each other.

Rising, she walked to the mirror and took a long look at her reflection. Face scrubbed bare of makeup. Damp, frowsy hair that was due for a trim and a root touch-up. A body that was headed downhill because she'd been too busy with Zac to go to the gym. Add a wardrobe left over from her college days, and the picture wasn't a pretty one. She was hardly the sort of woman who could hold the interest of a man like Emilio Santana.

Zac was tottering between pieces of furniture, taking a step or two, then grabbing whatever was handy to steady his balance. "Mama?" He looked up at her for approval. When she smiled, he grinned and held out his arms.

"Come here, you little monkey!" Grace scooped him up and hugged him. At least somebody loved her unconditionally.

Emilio had asked her to stay. What did that mean? Surely not marriage. She had no doubt he'd be a good father to his brother's son. But he would also want children of his own— children he knew she couldn't give him.

Setting Zac down again, Grace rummaged through the wardrobe for a presentable blouse to go with her jeans. She looked forward to riding with Emilio. But every hour she spent with him would be bittersweet. She had no doubt that she loved him—but love alone would never be enough.

Firing Pablo was bound to be an ugly business. But it needed to be done. Not only was he using his employer's property for seduction; he was lazy and unreliable, with a manner that skated the edge of insolence. It was all far too reminiscent of the man Emilio used to be. Evicting him from the Santana estate would be like Emilio sending his scandalous past away, as well.

Yes, it was time, Emilio told himself as he strode back toward the pool house. Dolores knew a good man from the village who needed the work, so replacing Pablo shouldn't be a problem. It would be a relief to have him gone.

The sun was up, high time for Pablo to be working, but there was no sign of him outside. Annoyed, Emilio flung open the pool house door. He found Pablo snoring in the hammock he kept in the back.

As the sun struck his face, Pablo opened his eyes. "Hello, boss," he said with a lazy grin. "Sorry to be late getting started. Wild night last night, if you know what I mean."

The rascal was incorrigible. "You won't be getting started today," Emilio said, reaching into his pocket. "Here's your back pay. Take your things and get off the property."

Pablo swung his legs to the floor and stood. Scratching his rear with one hand, he put the cash in the pocket of his khaki shorts even as he spoke out in protest.

"You're firing *me,* boss? But what for? Have I done something wrong?"

"Don't make me draw you a picture," Emilio growled. "Ask your brother. He got fired for the same reason."

Pablo yawned and ran a hand through his curls. "That pretty blonde gringa friend of yours might not be too happy about my going."

"What are you talking about?" Emilio sensed the fellow was baiting him. But his fury was a gut response, ignited by the mention of Grace.

Pablo grinned. "Why d'you think I needed my sleep this morning? I had her yowling like a cat in heat all night. She couldn't get enough of me. We were doing it more ways than you could—"

A grunt of pain ended the words as Emilio's fist cracked into his jaw.

Twelve

Riding behind Grace on the narrow trail, Emilio feasted his eyes on the hourglass curve of her waist and the fit of her jeans on her shapely rump. She sat the saddle with confidence, looking as if she could easily handle a more spirited horse than Manso. But she'd grown attached to the gray gelding and Emilio knew better than to push her.

Shifting the reins in his hand, he winced. His bruised knuckles would be tender for a day or two. But he wasn't sorry he'd smashed his fist into Pablo's chin. The bastard had deserved more than a cracked jaw for the ugly lie he'd told, a lie Emilio would have seen through even if he hadn't known the truth—that Grace had spent the night with *him*.

Pablo had slunk off like a whipped dog. He and his brother would have no trouble charming themselves into a new situation, probably with some gullible woman. But they were no longer his problem. He was well rid of the pair.

What had caught him off guard was the flash of rage the

lie had triggered. His woman had been slandered, and he'd
lashed out to defend her honor. Pablo had been lucky to get
away in one piece.

Emilio had been hesitant to tell Grace about the incident.
But in the spirit of honesty he'd related it on the way to the
stable.

"We're well rid of him," she'd replied, describing her own
encounters with the pool boy. "I don't want Zac growing up
around a man like that." For a moment, Emilio felt stung
at the words. Then he reminded himself that he wasn't that
kind of man anymore—that all of his own unsavory behavior was in the past. Just as Pablo and his brother were in the
past, never to trouble the Santanas again.

"If I'd known he'd approached you, I'd have pounded him
within an inch of his life," Emilio had responded with a
growl. "I hope I never see the lying bastard again."

Putting the unpleasantness behind them, they'd set out to
enjoy the rest of the day. For their afternoon ride he'd chosen a trail that wound through hills to a trickling waterfall. It
was a charming spot, a good place for quiet talk if he could
manage to put his thoughts into words.

Meanwhile he could enjoy the sight of her—happy and
laughing on horseback, the warm sun glinting on her gold-
streaked hair. He'd known many beautiful women, most of
them preoccupied with their own attractiveness. But Grace
was beautiful to the bone—all the more so because she
seemed unaware of it.

They reached the waterfall, dismounted and tethered the
horses to graze. The water was too cold for a swim but there
were shaded boulders, carpeted with moss, where they could
sit and enjoy the cooling mist. Emilio had brought two bottles
of chilled mineral water in an insulated pouch. He opened
one and passed it to Grace.

"Was it hard, making yourself ride again?" he asked her.

"Only at first. After that it was like I'd been doing it all along." Reaching out, she laid a hand on his. "Thank you. I could never have done it without your encouragement."

"Thank *you*. If you'd refused to try, we wouldn't be here now."

"This is lovely, isn't it?" Turning away, she watched the play of water over the rocks. In the silence, Emilio gathered his courage. He'd never been shy around females, but right now he felt like a twelve-year-old about to ask for his first dance.

He cleared his throat. "I want more time with you, Grace. Time to explore this relationship and see where it goes."

She turned back to him with startled eyes. What was she thinking? Had he just made a jackass of himself?

Awkward seconds passed before she spoke. "Would you care to explain what you just said?"

He exhaled, feeling awkward. "I care for you, Grace. And I'd like to believe you feel something for me. But we're both cautious people. We want to do the right thing—for ourselves and for Zac."

"I assume this isn't a marriage proposal." Grace looked cynical. Something told him she wasn't going to make this easy.

"Not yet. But if it turns out to be what we both want, marriage could be the next step."

"And if it doesn't turn out to be what we both want?"

"Then I hope we could at least stay friends."

Emilio felt as if he'd stepped in quicksand and was sinking with every word. He adored this woman. Why couldn't he just tell her instead of rattling on like a character in a bad novel?

She glanced down at her hands, then back at him. "Have you forgotten something, Emilio?" she asked softly. "I can't give you children."

"I know. I've thought of that." And he had, for most of the

morning. "Zac is my own flesh and blood. Once I formalize the adoption, he'll be my legal son—yours, too, if we marry. I could be perfectly content with one child."

"But what if—God forbid—something were to happen to Zac? Or what if you changed your mind and wanted more children—children of your own?"

The unspoken part of her message hung between them. There was no way she'd tolerate his having children with a mistress, as some men did.

Capturing her free hand, he pressed it to his lips. He could feel the pulse in her wrist racing like a little runaway watch.

"Grace, we aren't going to solve all of life's problems this afternoon. Let's give this time, enjoy each other's company and see what happens. Tomorrow I'd like to leave Zac here and drive you into Cusco for the day. I know you went shopping there, but there's so much more to see. There's nothing I'd like better than to be your guide."

She seemed to hesitate. Her smile, when it came, was like the sun peering from behind a cloud—a cloud that remained stubbornly in place. "All right. It sounds like a grand adventure. But for now we'd best be getting back to the house. Eugenia's watching Zac, and I told her we wouldn't be long."

Emilio led on the way back, conscious of her presence trailing behind him. She wasn't saying much but then, he'd given her a great deal to think about.

Had he said the right things or had his clumsy declaration left a disaster in its wake? Emilio enjoyed romantic games with women and prided himself on his skill with pretty words. But this was no game. This time he was gambling with his heart.

Giving Manso his head, Grace trusted the gray gelding to follow the stallion. If only she could trust her own emotions as easily. Wasn't this what she'd hoped for—a sign from

Emilio that he wanted to take their relationship beyond the "no strings attached" stage? She should be bubbling with excitement. Instead she felt...what? Deflated? Worried? Scared?

If only he'd told her he loved her. Instead he'd hedged his bets, presenting her with what amounted to a business proposition. They would spend some time together. If things went well, they might consider marriage. Or not.

It had been all she could do to keep from pummeling his chest and railing at him like a harpy, demanding that he love her.

Maybe it was the way he'd been raised. In his traditional, upper-class world, marriage was often a matter of convenience, an arrangement that had little to do with romantic love. In Emilio's eyes, his declaration would have been entirely proper. A woman like Mercedes Villanueva might have understood and accepted that. But for Grace it wasn't enough. She needed Emilio's love, not only for herself but for Zac.

Without that love they could never become a family.

They left for Cusco the next morning under a sky still streaked with dawn. This time Emilio had elected to do the driving himself—in a black vintage E-Type Jaguar with the top down. Grace huddled low in the seat, her jacket buttoned to her throat, her hair streaming in the wind. Emilio had switched on the heater to warm her legs, but the morning air was still chilly enough to make her shiver.

He flashed her a grin. "Once the sun comes up you'll be peeling off that jacket. Meanwhile, lean back and enjoy the view. You'll understand why we're going topless today."

Taking his advice, Grace adjusted the seat to an angle, giving her a panorama of terraced hillsides, wooded slopes and towering snowcapped peaks painted in sunrise hues. "Beautiful," she murmured. "It makes me want to start painting again. As soon as you have time to find me a studio—"

"Your studio's been cleared out and ready for a week," Emilio said. "North windows for the best light, a work table, an easel, a cupboard for your supplies and your own computer. When I get the new satellite dish hooked up, your internet access should be as good as it was in Arizona."

She stared at him, flabbergasted. "And you didn't tell me? Why?"

"I wanted to surprise you with it—*after* you asked."

"I've thought about asking. But I assumed you were too busy to be bothered."

His right hand moved from the gearshift knob to rest briefly on her knee. "When I said I wanted you to stay, I meant it, Grace. Now more than ever."

Grace swallowed the tightness in her throat. Emilio hadn't shared her bed last night. Her assumption had been that they both needed their rest. Now she wondered if he'd been waiting to be invited back, or if he'd just wanted to give her time to think about his offer. She'd given up trying to second-guess him. At this point in their relationship, only one thing was certain. Behind the facade of the tabloids, *the Peruvian Playboy* was a man of passion, generosity and complex emotions—a man she could love for the rest of her life, if she could only trust that that love would be returned.

As they wound upward into the thin, clear air of Cusco, the road became crowded. Buses and taxis vied for space with tradespeople on their way to market. Everywhere there were things to see. They passed a caravan of llamas loaded with bundles of hand-woven blankets. A woman in bright native dress trudged along the roadside, a baby on her back and a glorious bouquet of white calla lilies in her arms. Other women carried baskets on their heads—baskets filled with corn and squash, fresh fruits, even live chickens. Dark-eyed little girls, dressed like their mothers, carried burdens of their own. The boys, most of them in jeans and T-shirts, played tag among the crowd.

"You're looking at the real Peruvians," Emilio said. "When my ancestors came from Spain in the 1500s, they found a civilization more advanced than their own, and they did everything to destroy it. These people descended from the survivors. You've seen the terraces they built. Today you'll see more."

Emilio was a fascinating guide. Grace did her best to relax and put aside the awareness of why he'd brought her here. Their future could be riding on the outcome of this day—a prospect that both thrilled and frightened her.

Grace had studied the basics of Peruvian history in school. Now she was seeing the capital of the Inca Empire, where betrayals and battles had taken place. She was walking the cobbled streets and touching the massive stones, cut by Inca craftsmen to fit so precisely that no mortar was needed. Left in place after the Spanish conquest, these stones formed the foundations for everything from five-hundred-year-old churches to modern hotels, shops and restaurants.

They ate lunch in a small outdoor café off the Plaza de Armas. The food was simple and wholesome—savory beans and rice, fresh vegetables and fruit, served with white cheese and incredible crusty bread. Strolling musicians serenaded them with haunting native music played on panpipes, flutes and drums.

"I was starved!" Grace downed the last morsel on her plate and sipped her sherry. "You walked my legs off this morning, Emilio. How much more is there to see?"

"It would take weeks to see it all. But if your legs need a rest, our next stop's on a hill overlooking the city. We can drive there. Sacsayhuamán's not to be missed."

"Sacsay—*what?*"

Emilio laughed. "Sexy woman, as the tourists would say.

It's what's left of the Inca fortress that guarded the city. The Spaniards hauled off most of the stone for building, but they couldn't take the foundations. You'll see why."

Indeed, she did see why. The walls of the fort, laid out in a zigzag line, had been built on huge flat-sided boulders, some the size of small houses. Each one had been shaped to fit precisely against its neighbors like pieces of a giant jigsaw puzzle.

"How on earth did the Incas do that?" Grateful for a chance to rest, Grace sat next to Emilio on a stone bench. The spot gave them a sweeping view of the city below. "How could they even move rocks that size, let alone fit them so perfectly?"

"Nobody knows. That's the wonder of it, and the beauty." Emilio slipped an arm around her, allowing her head to fall against his shoulder. His lips brushed her hairline in a fleeting caress. "Do you think you could be happy raising Zac in my country, Grace?"

Her pulse leaped. *I could be happy with you anywhere in the world,* she thought. But what she said was, "Your country is amazing. I could certainly be happy here. But whether I *would* be depends on other conditions."

"Well said." His arm tightened in a quick, hard hug. "In the spirit of the day, I won't ask what those conditions are." Releasing her, he stood. "Since the afternoon's getting on, what do you say we head back? I have one more stop to make on the way out of town. Something personal. I hope you won't mind."

"Of course not." She let him help her to her feet and took his arm going down the hillside to the car. It was a relief to sink into the soft leather seat while Emilio paid the man he'd hired to watch the Jaguar. Minutes later they were headed for the main road.

They were nearing the outskirts of Cusco when Emilio

slowed the car and turned on to a side road. Since he'd said his errand was personal, Grace hadn't asked what it was. But by now she'd begun to be curious.

The road was paved, the neighborhood quiet. Emilio seemed lost in thought as they approached a high stone wall with a wrought-iron gate. Near the entrance, women in make-shift booths were selling small figurines of saints, miniature crosses and bouquets of flowers. Only then did the realization strike her—this place was a cemetery.

Emilio parked the Jaguar in the shade and nodded to the guard who came forward with an offer to watch it. "I try to visit my family whenever I'm in the country," he said to Grace. "If you're tired you're welcome to wait in the car. But if you want to come along, you might find this place interesting."

"Certainly I want to come." Maybe a visit to Emilio's departed family would give her some insight into what made this perplexing man tick.

Emilio bought a bouquet of creamy white lilies, which Grace offered to carry. Holding the flowers gently, so as not to bruise them, she walked beside him through the rusting iron gate.

The cemetery was unlike anything she'd ever seen. Instead of graves with headstones, the caskets were stacked above ground, six high, in row upon row of glass-fronted compartments. There were thousands of these compartments, more than Grace could begin to count. Glancing through some of the little glass doors, she saw that behind each one was a place for remembrances—photographs, fresh flowers, small mementos of the loved one's life. Here and there she saw people standing before open doors, cleaning and rearranging the displays. Others stood with heads bowed in prayer.

"It's the duty of family members to visit here every few

weeks," Emilio explained. "I'll need to come more often, since there's no one else."

Grace inhaled the subtle scent of the lilies she carried. "This isn't what I'm used to. But what a lovely custom. I can see the devotion in these displays. Where's your family?"

"Back there." Emilio glanced toward the rear of the compound, where several mausoleums rose against the wall. The grandest and most ornate of these bore the chiseled name *SANTANA,* flanked by marble angels, above the entrance.

Even on this warm day the crypt was chilly. Grace shivered as Emilio led her inside. Here the coffins—and there were many—were ensconced in niches and sealed behind marble slabs. The more recent ones featured narrow shelves for flowers and other mementos.

"The early Santanas were buried under the cathedral," Emilio said. "But the remains in here go back to the early 1800s. Here's my father."

Grace studied the portrait etched into the slab. "He looks very stern," she said.

"He was, so far as I could tell." Emilio laid a flower on the shelf. "Thinking back, I realize I barely knew him. He spent most of his time in Lima. Even when he was home, he didn't want to be bothered by noisy children, so we were kept out of sight."

"Sad," Grace murmured as Emilio moved on.

"My mother…" Emilio laid the second lily in its place. "You know her story. And over here is Arturo."

Grace gazed at Arturo's final resting place. The thin layer of cement that held the slab in place still looked fresh. What a tragic end for a man who was still young. "When Zac is older you can bring him here," she said. "He'll want to know about his father."

"Yes, but there's time yet." Emilio laid two lilies on the shelf. Was one on Zac's behalf, or perhaps for Cassidy's memory? "And here below him is Roberto, my other brother." Emilio had to kneel to place the last lily, but he took his time. Grace could sense the tenderness in him.

"How old was Roberto?" she asked.

"Four when he died. I wasn't much older than Zac at the time. The few memories I have of him are just impressions."

"What was wrong with him? Do you know?"

"Our family doctor, who treated Roberto, is still practicing in Cusco. Years later, based on what he remembered, he read up on current research into a newly identified medical condition and passed his findings on to Arturo. All I have to go on is what Arturo told me."

By now they'd stepped out of the mausoleum and into the glare of the afternoon sun. Momentarily blinded, she took his arm as he continued. "The doctor believes that what Roberto had was a rare, inherited condition called glycogen storage disease."

"I've heard of it." Grace felt an unexplained chill. "A friend of mine was a pediatric nurse. She mentioned a patient, a little girl, who had a form of it. She seemed fine for the first year of her life. Then her body lost the ability to process glucose. It took a terrible toll on her liver, her muscles and her brain. By the time she died, she'd wasted away to almost nothing." Grace paused as the fear crept over her. "You say the disease is inherited?"

"That's what Dr. Allende told Arturo. Of course, the diagnosis was made long after Roberto's death. There's no way to be certain it's even what Roberto had."

"But if that's what it was, and if it's inherited—" Her fingers tightened hard on his arm. "Emilio, we need to find out more. And we need to get Zac tested—right away."

Thirteen

Dr. Augustín Allende had been looking after the Santana family's health for as long as Emilio could remember. What the man lacked in specialty training, he made up in wisdom, discretion and an understanding of his patients.

Spurred by Grace's alarm, Emilio had telephoned him from the cemetery. Though he was now in semiretirement, the doctor had agreed to see them immediately.

They'd met with him in the medical office attached to his comfortable house. In his mid-seventies, he was an erect, vigorous man with sparse white hair and piercing eyes behind thick spectacles. He listened quietly while Emilio filled him in on the reason for their concern about Zac.

"Of course, we can't be certain what disease Roberto had," the doctor said. "Back then not much was known about his kind of illness, especially here in Peru. The poor child simply wasted away and died. There was no help for him.

"I only remembered him last year when I read a descripion of type IV glycogen storage disease, known as Andersen's disease, in a medical journal. The symptoms—early childhood onset, distended liver, wasting muscles, loss of brain function—matched Roberto's exactly."

Emilio glanced at Grace. She sat on the edge of her chair, hands clasping the wooden arms so tightly that the knuckles were white. She had to be thinking of her precious Zac, dying by slow degrees.

"That was when I contacted Arturo," the doctor continued. "I suggested that, since he was about to be married, he might want to be tested for the gene. But nothing ever came of it. And now...he has a son."

The doctor glanced toward Grace. "Let me allay your fears, Miss Chandler. I agree we should have the boy tested. But this illness is extremely rare. The gene that triggers it is recessive. For the disease to occur, it has to come from *both* parents."

"Both?" Grace's puzzled glance shifted from the doctor to Emilio.

Emilio cleared his throat. "What Dr. Allende hasn't mentioned, Grace, is that my mother and father were second cousins."

Grace looked as if the wind had been knocked out of her. Emilio could only hope the expression on her pale face was relief. "Let me make sure I understand," she said. "Roberto inherited the disease because the gene ran in the family, and both parents carried it."

The doctor nodded. "In theory at least, that's right."

"But with the same parents, why wouldn't Arturo and Emilio have been sick?"

"Because they were lucky." Reaching for a pen, he began sketching on a notepad—circles and lines showing patterns of inheritance. "See? Both parents were carriers, meaning that they had one normal gene and one gene for Andersen's.

With each child, they could have contributed either gene. It's like tossing two coins at the same time. The child who gets the two damaged genes has the disease. With one bad gene and one normal, the child is fine but still a carrier. Two normal genes and the problem goes away."

Emilio was intrigued. "So, since Arturo wasn't sick, that leaves two chances in three of his carrying the gene."

The doctor nodded. "And if he had it, there'd be a fifty percent chance of passing the gene to his son. But unless Zac's mother passed it on as well—and the odds of that are infinitesimal—the boy shouldn't be in danger." He shrugged. "Of course, if I'm wrong about Roberto's illness, everything I've told you is out the window. There may be no connection to Zac at all."

"Assuming you're right, Zac could still be a carrier," Emilio said. "For that matter, so could I. Maybe we should both be tested."

The doctor adjusted his glasses. "That's not a bad idea. There's a new lab in the capital that does genetic testing. Bring the boy in. I'll take DNA samples from both of you and send them there. I assume you'll want urgent priority."

"Of course, and I'll pay whatever it takes."

"Certainly." Rising, the doctor turned toward Grace. "I met your stepsister when she was here, Miss Chandler. Arturo brought her in with a fever. I took a blood sample and checked it for malaria, but the problem turned out not to be serious. A lovely young woman. I was sorry to hear of her loss."

"Thank you, Doctor." Grace rose and shook his hand. "I'll bring Zac's medical records the next time we come, so you can get his history. So far he's been a healthy little boy."

"As I'm quite sure he'll continue to be."

Emilio thanked the doctor for seeing them on short notice

and walked with Grace toward the exit. In the doorway, she suddenly turned back.

"One more question, Doctor. What if we get the worst news? What if Zac turns out to have Andersen's disease?"

The doctor hesitated, then shook his head. "The odds of that aren't worth worrying about, Miss Chandler. Go home and put it out of your mind."

Grace was silent all the way to the car. But as Emilio slid into the driver's seat, he glanced toward her and saw that she was trembling.

"You heard the doctor, Grace," he said. "Zac's fine. There's practically no chance that he inherited Roberto's illness."

Her hands clasped and unclasped in her lap. "I know what the doctor said. What I heard loud and clear is what he *didn't* say. There's no cure. If Zac is ill, we won't be able to save him. He'll waste away and die, just like Roberto."

Her voice broke as she battled tears. Emilio turned in his seat. Grace's worries were unfounded—he felt sure of that. Should he try to talk some sense into her? Should he tell her she was overreacting and that Zac was bound to be all right? If he could convince her, he'd be doing her a favor.

But looking into her stricken eyes, he knew better than to try. Grace's fear was a mother's fear—bone deep, born of instinct and a love stronger than reason. Zac's condition, good or bad, was beyond her control, and she knew it. She was in a state of helpless despair.

There was just one thing to do. Emilio reached out over the gear box and gathered her into his arms.

She huddled against him, quaking with dry sobs. He held her with awkward tenderness, his hands stroking her back, her shoulders, her hair. "It's all right, Grace," he murmured. "I understand that you're scared. But know that whatever happens, we'll get through it together. I'll be with you and Zac, all the way."

As he spoke the words, Emilio knew they were true. He wanted a life with this woman and the child they both cared for. There was no more hesitation, no more uncertainty on his part. It was as if Grace and Zac had already become his family.

Her tears were spilling over. Emilio could feel the wetness through his shirt. But at least she seemed calmer now. "I'm sorry," she whispered. "You must think I'm a hysterical fool. But the thought of Zac suffering the way your brother suffered…" She drew a painful breath. "I can't even imagine what your mother must have gone through."

Emilio's arms tightened around her. He had only faint memories of Roberto's death. But he recalled his mother's heavy alcohol use for the rest of her life. Strange, it had never occurred to him that his brother's illness might have been the start of it.

"We'll be all right," he murmured, holding her close. "We'll *all* get through this fine."

"My head tells me you're right. But my heart…" She pulled away from him and fastened her seat belt. "I know the doctor told me not to worry, but I won't relax until the tests are done and we know the results. Let's go home now, Emilio. I need to be with Zac. I need to see him and hold him."

"I think maybe I do, too." Emilio started the car and headed back toward the main road. The sun was low in the sky, but the traffic was flowing smoothly. With luck they'd be home before dark.

Grace closed her eyes, letting the breeze blow her hair and cool her warm face. Strange, how the day had started as a fun outing and ended with a crisis she could never have predicted. She would insist that they take Zac back to the doctor in the next few days. She'd been told there was little reason for concern, but she couldn't stand the uncertainty much longer. What if Zac turned out to have a double set of the deadly genes? Was there treatment available in the U.S.? Would it do any good to take him back?

"Are you all right?" Emilio had been unusually quiet.

"I will be." She forced herself to sound calm. "After all, this isn't about me. It's about Zac—and you. You're going to be tested, too. Are you concerned for yourself?"

"More curious than concerned. If I don't father any children, the gene shouldn't be an issue either way."

She willed herself not to dwell on his words. Right now the question of their future was the least of her worries.

"You say your parents were second cousins?"

"Yes. Do you find that strange?"

"A little. That wouldn't usually happen where I come from, even though it's legal."

"Here, in my parents' generation, it wasn't all that unusual. It was a matter of keeping the Santana bloodline pure and the wealth safely in the family. Now, of course, we know that wasn't such a good idea."

Grace was struck by a sudden thought. "What about Mercedes? Is she a relative?"

"A distant one, maybe. I haven't paid much attention to the Santana pedigree but our families were always close. We played together as children."

"I think she wants to marry you." The comment slipped out unchecked.

Emilio kept his eyes on the road. "Mercedes is a practical woman. I can understand her expecting me to step in and replace Arturo. But I have no reason to think she loves me. She's more like a sister than a possible wife. Besides—" He steered the Jaguar around a slow-moving truck. "I just might have someone else in mind for that job."

His last remark triggered a quickening of Grace's pulse. A few hours ago she'd have been thrilled to hear those words. But while Zac's fate hung in the balance, she couldn't let herself be distracted—not even by the thought of marrying Emilio.

"Was Mercedes in love with Arturo?" she asked, picking up the thread of the conversation.

"I can't say, since I wasn't around for their engagement. But it was what both families had planned on since they were children. What nobody expected was for Arturo to fall in love with Cassidy. When she left, I think he just resigned himself to doing his duty."

"What dismal prospects for a marriage."

"Maybe that's one reason the wedding never took place."

"Poor Mercedes." Grace's sympathy for the woman was real. For all her beauty, wealth and confidence, Mercedes had yet to find love. That she would offer Grace money and aid to leave the country showed how desperate she must be.

And there was something else. "You said Mercedes might be a distant relative. Do you think there's any chance she might carry the gene for Andersen's disease?"

"Who knows? Dr. Allende may have suspected it. That might have been why he urged Arturo to be tested before the wedding."

They were coming into Urubamba. By now rain clouds were moving in and the sky was getting dark. Lights from the hotels and restaurants glowed in the twilight. Tourists in hiking gear strolled along the main street, wandering in and out of the bars.

Grace found herself counting the minutes until the car passed through the gate and pulled up to the house. She ached to hold Zac and feel the warmth of his sturdy little body in her arms. She wanted to look into his bright button eyes and hear his childish voice chirping, "Mama!" Maybe then she'd start to believe everything would be all right.

Cassidy had gone through so much suffering to bring this child into the world. He was so precious, so loved. There had to be more to his life than an early, tragic end.

Thunder boomed across the sky as Emilio pulled the car up to the front entrance. Leaving the key in the ignition for Francisco, he helped Grace out of the car and followed her into the house. Eugenia was waiting in the front hall with a fussing Zac. Her young face wore a worried expression.

"He has fever," she said in her halting English.

Zac's whimpers rose to wails as he saw Grace. She rushed forward and swept him into her arms. When she turned back toward Emilio her eyes were wide with alarm. "He's burning up!"

Emilio felt his heart drop. As the youngest in his family, he'd never been around a sick baby. But judging from Grace's expression, a fever must be something serious.

"Is there a doctor close by?" she asked.

"Not one I'd trust. And in the dark, with a storm moving in, the road to Cusco isn't safe. That's how Arturo died, coming home late in the rain." As a stricken look crept over her face he added, "Dolores will have gone home for the day, but she lives in the village. She's good with sick children. I could send Eugenia for her."

Grace hesitated, then shook her head. "Don't bother her yet. I've got some baby drops that should help the fever. We can make Zac comfortable and keep an eye on him, then take him to Dr. Allende in the morning." The fear in her eyes deepened. "Emilio, you don't think—"

"No, of course not." He was able to read her thoughts because his had been the same. "Dr. Allende didn't say anything about fever."

"No…you're right. I don't recall that he did." She pressed her cheek to Zac's flushed forehead. He was clinging to her, still fussing. "I'll get those drops down him. A cool bath should help him feel better. If we can get him to sleep…"

Without finishing the sentence, she hurried down the hall toward her bedroom. Emilio took a moment to speak with Eugenia, asking her to spend the night in the small bedroom off the kitchen in case she was needed later to fetch Dolores. When he found Grace again she was giving Zac a sponge bath in the nursery. "I took his temperature with the thermometer I brought," she said. "It's almost 103—that's Fahrenheit, and it's high. He's a sick little boy. I can only hope this will make him feel better."

Zac appeared to enjoy the bath, but he was far from his usual mischievous self. He lay quietly, allowing Grace to dress him in a fresh diaper and clean pajamas. But when she turned down the light and laid him in his crib he began to cry.

Grace picked him up again. The dim light etched weary shadows on her face. "I can tell he wants to be rocked. This could be a long night." She glanced at Emilio. "You might as well go to bed."

"You're the one who looks worn out," Emilio said. "Let me try rocking him while you get some rest. We can trade off later." When she looked hesitant he added, "You wanted me to practice being a father. Here's my chance."

"Fine. Sit down." Her voice was thready with exhaustion. "If it doesn't work, I'll hear and come back."

Emilio sank into the rocking chair and settled the fussing baby against his shoulder. "We'll make it work, won't we, Zac," he muttered.

Zac's only response was to fuss louder and bang his head against Emilio's collarbone. Grace watched them from the doorway. "Remember, it helps to rock him," she said.

"Get some sleep." Emilio cradled the hot little body closer

and began to rock. The chair had a creak in its ancient joints. The rhythmic sound was oddly soothing. Little by little Zac began to relax. His head settled into the hollow of Emilio's shoulder. What was the lullaby Grace had sung? Emilio couldn't remember the words or the melody. Instead he began singing softly in Spanish. The song was a love ballad, not a lullaby, but Zac seemed to like it.

Solamente una vez, a mí en la vida... Solamente una vez, y nada mas...

A sense of bliss crept over Emilio. Beneath his hand he felt the rise and fall of each breath and the subtle beating of the baby's heart. This child was so precious, so vulnerable. There was nothing he wouldn't do to protect him, nothing he wouldn't sacrifice to give him a better life.

Was this how it felt to be a father?

The next morning Zac's fever was down. He felt well enough to drink some juice and eat some banana slices. Emilio had Francisco bring the big car around and buckle the baby seat into the back. By the time the early traffic had thinned out, they were on the road to Cusco.

The doctor took Zac's temperature and checked his eyes, ears, throat and lungs. "I don't see any cause for worry," he said. "Zac appears to be getting over the fever on his own. I'll prescribe some more drops in case he needs them. Give him plenty of fluids, and he should be fine."

Grace felt the rush of relief. "So this fever has nothing to do with—"

"Absolutely not. As far as I can tell, Zac's a healthy little boy. But I know you won't stop worrying until we have those test results. So let's take care of that now."

After taking swabs from Zac and Emilio, the doctor sealed the samples for the lab. "I'll get these out today, top priority," he said. "We should hear back in the next week. I'll call you as soon as the news arrives. Meanwhile, relax and stop worrying. I can almost guarantee everything will be fine."

"*Almost*. That's a very big word." Grace thanked the doctor and gave him the copies she'd made of Zac's birth certificate and medical history. Then she walked out beside Emilio as he carried Zac to the car.

"The doctor's right, Grace," he said. "Everything's going to be fine. We should put this out of our minds until we hear from him."

"I know." Grace sighed. "I've probably driven you crazy with my fretting. As long as Zac's getting better, let's table the issue. Unless there's some good reason, we won't even talk about it. Agreed?"

"Agreed." His free hand squeezed her shoulder. "Let's make it a good week."

And so they tried, mostly by keeping busy. Emilio's new oversized satellite dish arrived in sections. He spent much of his time reading instructions and supervising the crew of semiskilled workmen he'd hired to assemble and install it.

Once Zac was feeling better Grace unpacked her art supplies and put them in her new studio. Emilio had chosen the perfect room and furnished it with everything an illustrator might need. There was even a play area for Zac. It should have meant the world that he wanted her to be pleased, and it did—she *was* pleased. But the uncertainty about Zac hung over her like a cloud. She forced herself to do some sketching and even phoned her publisher about new projects, including a children's picture book about Peru. But Zac was always in her thoughts. Even when he was napping or being cared for by the maids, she found herself dropping her work to run and check on him.

Only the nights kept them anchored. Their lovemaking had taken on a new tenderness and a new trust. By unspoken consent they held back talk of love and marriage while they waited for the test results. But the commitment was there, deeper and more binding than words.

The week was almost up when Emilio walked into Grace's studio. One look at his face and she began to tremble. The stick of charcoal she was using to sketch dropped from her shaking fingers.

"Dr. Allende's nurse just called me," he said. "The doctor has the test results and wants to speak with us in person."

"She didn't tell you what the results were?"

"She didn't know. But she did say there was no need to bring Zac with us."

"Then it's bound to be good news, isn't it?" Grace's heart was pounding.

"Of course it'll be good news."

"But why wouldn't he just tell you on the phone?"

"She said he wanted to speak with both of us. I've already asked Eugenia to watch Zac and ordered Francisco to bring the car around."

Grace wiped her hands on her smock. "I'll get my purse and meet you at the car," she said.

Emilio glanced at Grace as they took seats in the doctor's office. She'd been mostly silent in the car. Now she was taut and quivering like a bowstring. He'd known better than to try and reassure her. The doctor could have conveyed simple good news over the phone. Something was up.

The doctor walked in with a folder in his hand. He greeted them and sat down at his desk. "I know you've been anxious, so I'll get to the results right away," he said. "I'll start by saying that both Emilio and the baby are fine. Emilio, you won the coin toss. Your genes show no sign of Andersen's disease or anything else the lab could discover."

Grace's voice was a strained whisper. "What about Zac? Is he all right?"

"Zac is fine. No sign of Andersen's. He appears to be a healthy, normal child in every respect."

Grace's body slumped in relief.

"So why are we here?" Emilio asked the doctor. "Why did you want to see us today?"

The doctor opened the folder and pushed it across the desk. "The tests revealed something else. Zac's DNA profile was compared to yours, Emilio. It carried none of the same markers. I am sorry to upset you, but there is no denying the truth. The boy can't possibly be your brother's son. He's not even a member of your family."

Fourteen

The doctor spoke into the stunned silence. "I suspected the truth as soon as I compared Zac's medical history with the ones I had on file. Arturo's blood was Type O. So was Miss Miller's—I did a routine test when she was here. If they were his parents, then Zac's should have been the same. But the record you brought me shows his blood as Type B. If you know anything about heredity and blood types, you'll know why that didn't look right to me."

Grace couldn't bear to look at Emilio, but she could imagine the shock on his face. Would it turn to anger, directed at her? Would he think she'd been deliberately lying to him all along?

Struggling for composure, she found her voice. "Why didn't you tell us what you suspected, doctor?"

"Because at the time, I wanted to believe it was a mistake. I understand how much is riding on this child being the Santana heir. But the truth is right here." His index finger jabbed the paper with the test results. "Zac isn't Arturo's son."

"This doesn't make sense," Emilio said. "I saw a copy of Zac's birth certificate. Arturo is named as the father."

Grace spoke up, knowing her words could change everything between them. "That was my doing. Cassidy slipped into a coma soon after Zac was born. I was the one who furnished the information on the birth certificate, and I assumed Arturo was the father. I knew that listing his name would make the adoption harder, but I didn't want to make Zac wonder who his father was."

"Did Cassidy *tell* you he was the father?" Emilio's voice rasped with tension.

"She never said he wasn't. And she never mentioned anyone else. You saw the letter from your brother, Emilio. Even Arturo believed he was Zac's father."

"Did he? Or was he too proud to admit he didn't know?"

Grace recalled Arturo's terse letter, stipulating that Zac have no claim on his estate. Had the businesslike dismissal it contained been written at Mercedes's insistence, or had Arturo suspected, even then, that Zac wasn't his?

The doctor rose from his chair. "I can see the two of you have things to resolve. I've done my part. All I can do now is wish you a satisfactory solution."

A satisfactory solution? Grace stood, feeling as if the ground had crumbled away under her feet. What kind of solution could they hope for now?

They thanked the doctor for his services and walked outside to the car. It was a good thing Francisco would be at the wheel. After the shock he'd received, Emilio didn't trust himself to drive.

Grace huddled beside him in the backseat, probably braced for a tongue-lashing. But Emilio couldn't blame her for this mess. She'd made an honest mistake, and not in her own favor. If she'd listed Zac's father as "unknown," adopting the boy would have been simple. Instead, no thanks to his meddling, she'd had her whole life uprooted.

So what was going to happen now?

Impulsively, he reached out and laid his hand on hers. A muffled sob escaped her throat. Emilio was grateful for the glass that separated them from the driver, giving them a measure of privacy.

"I'm sorry, Emilio," she said. "I'm so sorry."

"Hush." He gathered her close. "Don't blame yourself, Grace. If I hadn't come knocking on your door, demanding my brother's child, none of this would have happened."

"What are we going to do?" she whispered.

"We'll just have to work that out. One thing I know. I don't want to lose you—or Zac."

"You're saying that now." She pushed away from him, and he saw the anguish in her face. "But Zac's no longer the heir you need. And I can't give you children, Emilio. The accident—do I need to draw you a picture? I had a hysterectomy at fifteen. The surgeons saved one ovary so I'd have the hormones, but they took everything else."

"I love you, Grace." He pulled her to him again. "I know this is a hell of a time to say it, but it's true."

"I love you, too. But given what we've learned, the most loving thing I could do would be to take Zac and go home to Arizona."

"Don't talk like that. We'll work things out."

"How? You're not thinking, Emilio. You could marry anyone else and have all the children you wanted. Even Mercedes—you heard the doctor, you don't have the gene for Andersen's disease. There'd be no problem with—"

"Stop it, Grace!" He curbed the impulse to seize her shoulders and shake her. "Let's give this a few days. Right now we're both too upset for any kind of decision."

She stared at him. Then something inside her seemed to

give way. "Oh, I suppose you're right. We're both in shock. Giving this time to sink in won't cause any harm."

Emilio brushed a kiss across her forehead. He loved this woman more than life. Right now that was the one certainty in this whole debacle.

She was silent for a few moments, resting against him. Then she surprised him with a shake of her head and a bitter chuckle. "That Cassidy! She was always full of surprises. What do you suppose she was thinking?"

"We'll never know, will we?"

"Maybe she *wanted* to get pregnant. She knew she was dying. She could have wanted to leave something of herself behind—and Arturo wouldn't cooperate."

"Or she was just feeling frisky and he wasn't around. I knew Cassidy, too. 'Impulsive' didn't begin to describe her."

"I think she loved Arturo. At least she said she did. But you're right. Knowing Cassidy, anything could've happened."

Emilio remembered the photo with the shattered glass he'd found in Arturo's desk. Arturo had been angry enough to strike at the picture, but he hadn't thrown it away. Had he known Cassidy was pregnant with another man's child? Had he discovered that she'd cheated on him? Or was it just her leaving that had driven him to the edge?

Arturo, proud man that he was, had never revealed a word.

So who was Zac's father?

"I don't suppose we'll ever know for sure," Grace replied when Emilio voiced the question. "To me, it doesn't matter. Zac is who he is. Cassidy still gave him to me. But I understand that you might feel differently. Do you want to know the truth?"

"I'm not sure. What good would it do to know?"

"Zac will want to know someday. Still…" Her voice trailed off into a wistful sigh. "What a mess! I'm so sorry, Emilio. If I'd known—"

"If you'd known, you wouldn't be here. I would never have met you and Zac. I would never have fallen in love with you."

"And you would have been better off."

"Hush. We're not going there now. Remember?" He kissed her gently. "Be still and get some rest. We'll be home soon."

As she settled against him, Emilio's thoughts were drawn back to the question gnawing at his mind. Who *had* fathered Cassidy's child?

Cassidy and several of her model friends had come with him to Urubamba. When the party had broken up and the others left, Emilio had left, too. Cassidy had stayed behind to spend a few more weeks with Arturo.

There'd been other men around the place, some of them young and attractive. Two of the models, Emilio recalled, had been male. He'd suspected they were gay, but he couldn't be sure. Arturo's friends had been in and out as well. Any one of them could have gotten Cassidy pregnant.

A woman like Cassidy—how could any man look at her and not desire her? Emilio had wanted her himself before she chose his brother. Whether she'd been looking for stud service or just a romp between the sheets, she could've had her pick of any man in sight.

He recalled how she'd spent much of her time around the pool, swimming and sunning, showing off her glorious body in that minuscule green bikini she liked to wear. Even now, he could picture her on the diving board, her sunlit hair a fiery cloud, laughing as she executed a perfect swan dive into the water. No man with eyes could have resisted watching her. No man who had seen her at that pool…

The answer to Emilio's question slammed into place with the force of a thunderclap.

By the time the car pulled up to the house it was midafternoon. Grace and Emilio had fallen into silence, both lost in their own thoughts—and knowing that nothing they could say would make things easier.

When Francisco opened the door, Grace climbed out of the car and hurried inside. Right now there was just one thing she needed—to be with Zac.

She entered her room to find Eugenia in the rocking chair, knitting. The girl smiled, put a finger to her lips and glanced toward the crib, where Zac lay fast asleep.

Gracias. Grace mouthed the word and indicated with a strained smile and a nod that Eugenia could leave. Alone, she stood by the crib, gazing down at Zac's sleeping face.

Now that she knew he wasn't Arturo's child, she had little doubt who'd fathered him. Cassidy had always been drawn to beautiful men—even those who, like Pablo, were sadly lacking in character. If she'd wanted a baby, and if Arturo had been unwilling or unable to father her child, she would have chosen the most splendid physical specimen she could find.

Zac was a perfect little boy with his mother's exquisite features, his father's melting brown eyes and his own sweet, mischievous nature. To Grace, it didn't matter how he'd come to be. He was hers and she loved him without reservation.

But what about Emilio? He was bound to guess the truth, if he hadn't guessed already. He might be willing to accept a stranger's child, or even the child of a friend. But how could he be a loving father to the son of a man he detested?

The very thought of putting Zac—and Emilio—through that kind of emotional wringer was enough to make her want to start packing. And she had yet to tackle the larger issue— Emilio's need for a Santana heir she couldn't give him.

If only, by some miracle, Emilio could love Zac the way she loved the boy—unconditionally, with no regard for his parentage. If only he could be content with their little budding family—just the three of them, together.

But she knew better than to hope. Emilio was a *man*—a

Latino man with all the fierce macho pride his heritage entailed. Arturo's death had destined him to become the patriarch of a powerful family, to breed vital new life into the Santana line.

With her as his wife, that would be impossible.

In the afternoon stillness, Grace could hear footsteps approaching down the hall. Her pulse quickened as she recognized their cadence. Was Emilio looking for her? Would he come into the nursery, smile down at the sleeping Zac and take her in his arms? Would his kiss reassure her that nothing had changed?

But she was fantasizing now. When the footsteps came closer, paused outside her door, and then faded into silence, she was heartsick—but she wasn't surprised.

Emilio's thoughts roiled as he strode down the hall. He'd been about to enter Grace's room when he realized he was in no condition to see her—or to see Zac. He needed time to adjust to this new reality. He could only hope Grace would understand and be patient with him.

Pablo—that lazy, insolent, rutting *cabrón*.

Had he been aware that Zac could be his son? Not likely, Emilio reasoned. Pablo hadn't seen that much of the boy. Even if he had, he might have assumed Zac was Grace's child—or if he'd heard the talk, he could've believed the boy was Arturo's.

Another question—had Arturo known Cassidy was cheating on him? If so, why hadn't he fired Pablo? Was it because keeping the pool boy employed was the only way to keep the scandal quiet? Given Arturo's pride, that made sense.

But what if Emilio's hunch was wrong? There was only one way to know for sure—find Pablo and ask him. Now that he'd been fired, the rascal should be only too happy to confess.

And then what? Emilio would never tell Pablo he had a son. He could only take what he knew and deal with it.

Pablo and Fermín lived in town, in their late mother's house. Emilio had never been to the place, but Ana and Eugenia had known the deceased woman. One of them should be able to give him directions.

If the truth about Zac's father was within reach, he couldn't walk away without knowing.

Zac was beginning to stir when Grace heard the mechanical growl of the Jaguar heading toward the gate. Only Emilio, as far as she knew, would be driving the sleek black sports car. Until today, it wouldn't have been like him to leave without telling her. But things were different between them now. How different, she had yet to learn.

Earlier, on the way home, he'd told her he loved her. She would have given anything to believe that those feelings would last under the weight of this new revelation. But Grace had known, even then, that he'd been in a state of denial. Now he was clearly in torment. Much as she loved Emilio, taking Zac home to Arizona might be the only way to give him peace.

Zac opened his eyes, saw her and smiled. "Mama!" he said. Grace's heart contracted. He was hers, her own darling boy; and no one would ever threaten to take him again. Back in Tucson she could finalize the adoption process, listing the father as unknown since there was no proof to the contrary. Zac would be her legal child. Nobody would care whether he was the son of a Peruvian billionaire or a womanizing pool boy.

And Emilio—he would be free to start the family he needed and become the man he was destined to be.

She would never stop loving him. But she would never see him again.

* * *

Even with Ana's directions, it took Emilio twenty minutes to find the house he was seeking. Situated at the end of an alleyway between a garage and a hardware shop, the small adobe structure was surprisingly well kept, with curtains at the windows and a child-sized swing in the yard.

Emilio stopped in front of the house and double-checked the address. This had to be the place, but it wasn't what he'd expected. After locking the car, he opened the flimsy gate and walked up to the front porch. Before knocking on the door, he hesitated. Maybe he'd come on a fool's errand. Pablo had lied about spending the night with Grace. He was capable of lying about Cassidy, too.

The door was opened by a young woman with a pretty but tired face. One hand balanced a baby against her shoulder. A small girl clung to her legs.

"You must be *Don* Emilio Santana," she said. "I recognize your car. But if you're looking for my brothers, Pablo and Fermín, they are gone. They left for Lima last week to find work."

A smile lit her weary face and Emilio realized that, like her brothers, she was very good-looking. "Please don't be sorry you fired them," she said. "I know they behaved badly. It was time for them to leave and be on their own." She gave a nervous little laugh. "Sorry, I've forgotten my manners. My name is María."

Emilio shook the thin, work-worn hand she offered. "They lived here with you?"

"With me and my husband. He works as a mechanic in the garage you passed. I love my brothers but things will be easier without them. They paid for nothing—no food, no rent. They acted as if they were kings."

Emilio glanced at the two children—beautiful children, with big, dark eyes. If his suspicions were true, they could be Zac's cousins. But that was something he'd never know. Tracking the brothers down in Lima would be like looking for two fleas on a shaggy dog.

On impulse, he fished for his wallet and pulled out a handful of bills. "I came here because I owed them this money," he lied. "Put it toward what your brothers should have paid you. And if your husband ever needs work, have him come and see me. I can always use a good mechanic."

María's eye grew huge as she counted the bills. "But this is too much! It's—"

"Never mind. I'm sure you earned that and more living with those two."

Before she could argue, Emilio took his leave, started the car and headed for the main road. He'd come here looking for answers. Instead, he'd been given more questions. How could the family that had spawned Fermín and Pablo produce a good woman like María? Could bloodline really determine a person's character, or was the idea just superstition?

As he drove homeward, Emilio was overcome by the need to be with Grace and make things right between them. He loved her. He wanted her, and nothing else mattered. Any problems they might have could be worked out over time.

Leaving the Jaguar outside for Francisco, he strode into the house and down the long corridor to Grace's bedroom. It occurred to him that he should have brought flowers—but that could wait. All he wanted now was to take her in his arms and hold her until the pain and shock eased for them both.

Her door was ajar. Aching with anticipation, he opened it and stepped into the room.

The first thing he noticed was that the wardrobe she'd used was open and empty, as were the dresser drawers. Grace stood beside the bed. Zac played next to her as she folded clothes into her open suitcase.

"What's going on here, Grace?" He stared in disbelief. There had to be some mistake.

She gave him a look of tired resignation. "I've thought this over carefully," she said. "For your sake, for Zac's, and even for my own, we can't stay here any longer. We're leaving, Emilio, and you have no right to stop us. Zac and I are going home to Tucson."

Fifteen

Grace rested her head against the window of the lumbering commercial jet, tired eyes blurring the cloudscape outside. Beside her Zac slept in his car seat, worn out after their tedious wait at the Lima airport. Emilio had offered to fly her home in his private plane or at least buy them first-class airline tickets. She'd refused both offers, maxing out her credit card for two seats in coach. Her privileged existence was over. The sooner she got that through her head, the better.

Long hours from now she and Zac would arrive in Tucson. After a few weeks of getting back to normal it would be as if their time in Peru had been a dream. Their lives would go on as if it hadn't happened at all. But she would never forget Emilio's reaction when he'd walked into her room and found her packing her suitcase. An ache rose in her throat as she relived the scene.

For an instant his face had reflected shock. Then, like the

first frost of autumn, his expression had hardened, transforming into an icy mask that hid whatever he might be feeling. Only then had he spoken.

"So you've made up your mind. It didn't take you long, did it?"

"Emilio—" She'd fought the urge to run to him and fling her arms around his neck. Would he respond, or would holding him be like embracing a granite statue?

The nightgown she'd been packing had twisted in her hands. "So help me, I've tried. I've racked my brain for some way to make this work. But there's no way. If I were to stay, you'd come to resent me for what I couldn't give you. You'd even come to resent Zac, an innocent little boy, because he didn't have your precious family blood. We have to leave. It's the only answer."

A muscle had twitched in his cheek, the only sign he'd understood. What had she hoped for? That he'd fall to his knees and beg her to stay, or maybe take her in his arms and kiss her till she changed her mind? She should have known that Emilio would be too proud to do either. He would never play the supplicant.

Not that she would have given in if he had. She was leaving Emilio for his own good—leaving because she loved him.

His gaze had softened as it lingered on Zac. Playing in the bedcovers, Zac had pulled the quilt over his head, peeked out from under the edge, grinned at him and giggled.

Emilio's throat had moved as if swallowing something hard and sharp. Tightening his jaw, he'd turned back toward Grace. "If that's what you want, I've no right to stop you," he'd said in a flat voice. "Since I brought you here, I owe you the trip home."

"You don't owe me a thing," she'd replied. "Since it's my decision to leave, I'll get us home by myself."

"Whatever you say. Let me know if you need my help."
He'd turned and walked out of the room, leaving her to fall
apart in silence.

The clouds outside had deepened to the color of washed
ink. Beside her, Zac stirred and whimpered. Grace rubbed his
belly and he settled back into sleep. Her mouth felt dry, her
eyes raw from sleepless nights and solitary tears. She craved
coffee but didn't want to risk waking Zac, who was bound
to be cranky, by summoning the flight attendant. Glancing
at her watch, she counted the remaining hours in the flight.

Emilio had made himself scarce in the three days it had
taken Grace to arrange her return trip. But he'd been help-
ful in ways she needed, pulling strings to get her on the con-
necting flight from Cusco and enlisting Francisco to pack
and ship a crate of her art supplies. He'd been kind but distant, avoiding Zac and making no effort to talk her into staying. Grace could only imagine how deeply she'd wounded
his pride.

That morning, before closing her suitcase, she'd slipped
the engraved gold bracelet into an empty dresser drawer. It
was too valuable to justify keeping and too laden with meaning to be worn again. If only she could leave her memories
behind as easily.

Saying goodbye had been a wrenching experience. Ana
and Eugenia had wept as they showered Zac with kisses.
Dolores, who'd seen far worse tragedies in her long life, had
remained stoic, as had Emilio. Having made excuses not to
accompany her to Cusco, he'd bidden her farewell with the
others at the house. With a stony expression, he'd rumpled
Zac's hair, then raised Grace's hand to his lips and brushed
a kiss across her knuckles.

"I won't forget you, Grace," he'd said. "If you change your

mind…" The rest of his words had trailed off, as if he'd regretted what he was about to say.

Choking on her reply, Grace had stumbled to the car. As Francisco drove her toward the gate, she'd willed herself not to look back.

Now it was night. The plane's engines droned in the darkness. Sleet from a passing storm spattered the windows. Ignoring the in-flight movie on the screen, Grace gazed down at Zac's blessedly sleeping face.

One thing might have persuaded her to stay in Peru. If Emilio had been willing to forget Zac's heritage and embrace the boy as his legal son, her decision could have been different. But she'd known that would never happen. Emilio's cool, distant silence when she'd told him her decision had spoken louder than any words he might have said.

She knew that in the upcoming nights she would lie sleepless, aching for the sound of his voice and the sweet, enfolding strength of his arms. But eventually she would move on. She had no choice except to build a life without him.

Emilio leaned against the paddock fence, one hand stroking the neck of the gentle gray gelding. "You miss her, don't you, Manso?" he murmured. "So do I, *viejo*. So do I."

In the weeks that had passed since Grace and Zac's departure, Emilio had flung himself into his work, revising production schedules, writing new business plans and putting unproductive properties up for sale. In addition to frequent video conferences, he'd flown into Lima twice to meet face-to-face with his board of directors. He'd sensed the new respect in their behavior toward him. He was El Jefe, the boss, firmly in charge. It felt good.

But he couldn't keep busy 24/7. Alone in the too-quiet house, the loss of the woman and child who might have become his family came back to haunt him. He'd known he would miss Grace. What surprised him was how much he missed Zac—the glint of mischief in those melting dark eyes, the endless curiosity, the weight of the sturdy little body in his arms. If he'd had a son of his own—the realization staggered him—he would have wanted the boy to be just like Zac.

No, not *like* Zac. Zac.

As for Grace, he seemed to see her everywhere. He caught himself listening for her footsteps on the tiles and for the sound of her voice. More than once he'd reached across the bed at night to draw her close, only to find the space empty.

When Ana discovered her gold bracelet in the drawer, he'd cradled it in his hands as if it still held her warmth. He'd wanted her to keep his gift. That she'd left it was one more sign of her resolve to make a clean break.

He'd never meant for her and Zac to go. But Grace's decision had been his own fault. He should have stepped up as soon as Zac's test results were known. Instead he'd turned his back, wanting to keep his ugly turmoil to himself. It had been the worst mistake of his life.

In the end, his pride had undone him. Grace had announced that she wanted to leave. And he—the Peruvian playboy who'd sworn he'd never beg a woman for anything— had let her.

Could he have accepted Zac as his son? At the time, he hadn't been sure. Now he knew better, but it was too late. Grace would never forgive him for the way he'd let her down.

"Hello, Emilio." The voice startled him. He glanced around to find Mercedes standing beside him at the paddock fence. Hair and makeup perfect, she was clad in a sleeveless white sheath. Her red stiletto heels had sunk partway into the grassy earth. "I heard Grace had left," she said. "But I thought I should wait a decent interval before coming over. Am I intruding?"

"No, of course not. I could use a friend right now." Offering his arm, he headed back toward the pool. She teetered along beside him in her high heels.

"A friend." Her sharp, bright eyes studied him. "That really is all you want from me, isn't it? You're in love with her, aren't you?"

"No comment."

"So why did you let her go?"

"It was her decision, not mine."

"And she took the boy. Since you would never have let her leave with Arturo's son, I take it you finally learned the truth."

"What?" Dropping his arm, he turned to stare at her. "You knew?"

"Let's say I suspected. One day, when Arturo wasn't here, I walked in on Cassidy and that beautiful pool boy. I told Arturo about them. That's why she left."

"She would have left, anyway. She knew she was dying and it seems clear she never planned to tell him."

"I didn't know that at the time. I just wanted Arturo back." She took his arm again. "I thought that was the end of it until you brought her son here. One look at that pretty child and it all fell together."

"At the party…I remember you saying Zac looked like his father."

"Yes. My little private joke."

"Why in God's name didn't you tell me?"

Mercedes shook her elegant head. "Arturo never forgave me for telling him about Cassidy. That may have been one of the reasons he never went through with our wedding. I was afraid you might feel the same way if I told you about that precious boy. I could only hope you'd find out on your own."

"So you kept it to yourself all this time." They'd reached

the flagstones that bordered the pool area. On solid ground now, Mercedes released his arm with a bitter chuckle.

"Oh, I had other tricks up my sleeve. Did you know I offered Grace a half million dollars to take the boy and leave? She turned me down. Her excuse was that she didn't want to take my money. But I knew, even then, that she was in love with you."

Facing him, she took both his hands in hers. "How well do we understand each other, Emilio?"

"Like brother and sister." It was true. They'd been friends for as long as he could remember.

She smiled, and there was something in that smile that he recognized, even though he hadn't seen it in years. Something that looked like the old gentle honesty they used to share as children. "You and I together—it seems the expected thing to do. But we both know it would never work, don't we? Especially not when you're in love with someone else, and she's in love with you."

"Mercedes—" Something tightened in his throat.

She squeezed his hands. "If you're not going to be with me then you might as well be with the one who makes you happy. Don't be a fool, *querido!* Go and get the woman before it's too late! Do whatever it takes to bring her back, or you'll be sorry for the rest of your life!"

Releasing him, she strode off in the direction of the drive. At the corner of the house, she paused and glanced back over her shoulder. "I can't imagine Grace thinks much of me," she said. "But tell her this. If she comes back, and if she chooses to forgive the past, she'll have a friend."

Emilio stood where she'd left him. Could he really do this? Swallow the Santana pride and beg Grace to come back to him? How could he make her listen? What could he say to her?

Then he remembered the night he'd come to claim Zac—the words she'd said to him. And he knew.

Grace had celebrated Zac's first birthday by going before the court. Now the adoption was final. Zac was her very own son and she was, at long last, his mother.

She was happy. But it was a bittersweet happiness. Emilio had made their little family complete in a way that it might never be again.

Tonight, as she cleaned up after supper, her thoughts wandered their familiar path back to Peru. She remembered Emilio's first diapering experience and the expression on his face as Zac soaked the front of his shirt. She recalled the sight of him playing peekaboo with Zac in the bed, both of them laughing. He would have made a wonderful dad. Maybe one day, thanks to her leaving, he would get his chance.

Sadly, it wouldn't be with her.

She was about to load the dishwasher when she realized Zac had wandered out of the kitchen, where he'd been playing. She'd baby-proofed the house as best she could. Still, with the little mischief walking, every second she took her eyes off him was a new invitation to disaster.

A crash sent her rushing to the living room. Her son was all right, thank heaven, but what a mess! Zac had managed to catch a tendril of the ivy plant she'd moved out of his reach. The brass pot he'd pulled down wasn't broken, but damp, black dirt streaked the rug and coated one delighted little boy.

Smudging the dirt on his face, he grinned up at her as if to say, *Wow, Mama! Look what I just did!*

Grace dropped to her knees beside him and began brushing off the worst of the grime. "Just look at you!" she muttered. "One thing I've got to say for you. You're all boy, Zac Chandler!"

"Ptthhtt!" He reached out, smeared dirt on her face and giggled.

Catching him close, she blew against his soft neck. "Now we'll both need a bath!" she said.

At that moment the doorbell rang.

"Talk about timing…" Leaving her son on the floor, Grace stumbled to her feet and opened the front door. Emilio stood on the threshold, a bemused expression on his tired face.

"Have I come at a bad time?" he asked.

Grace sagged against the wall, not knowing whether to laugh or cry. "You could've called," she managed to say.

"And have you avoid me?" His teasing smile vanished, replaced by a more serious expression. "If you'll let me in, I have something to say to you—both of you. After that, if you want me to, I'll leave and never bother you again."

Grace moved away from the door giving him room to enter. What did he want? To tear off another piece of her heart? Part of her wanted to lose herself in his arms. But saying goodbye the first time had been all she could do. How could he expect her to say goodbye again?

Zac had caught sight of Emilio. With a happy squeal, the boy flung himself against Emilio's legs, smearing his khakis with black dirt. Laughing, Emilio boosted him against his shoulder, smudging his shirt, as well. Zac reached up and streaked more dirt across his cheek.

"Does this mean I've joined the grubby face club?" Emilio joked.

Grace wasn't laughing. "My son is glad to see you," she said.

"Your son." Emilio's gaze warmed. "You've earned the right to say those words. Congratulations."

"I never expected to see you again, Emilio. What do you want?"

"First things first." His free hand drew her gold bracelet out of his pocket. "You left this behind."

Grace's throat tightened at the sight of the engraved bracelet. But she made no move to take it. It was a souvenir of a different world, a world she'd done her best to forget. "Maybe I wanted to leave it behind. Like you, it was never really mine." She forced back welling tears. "You mentioned you had something to say to us."

Emilio gave the bracelet to Zac, who seemed taken by his reflection in the polished surface. "I came to apologize, Grace. I should've been there for you the whole time. Instead I let you believe I'd turned my back. Worse, I was too proud to stop you from leaving. I was a fool. I want you to come home with me—you and Zac—as my wife and son."

Grace's knees threatened to give way. She sank onto the arm of a chair, seized by an irrational fear—the fear of *almost* getting what she wanted.

"You know I can't give you children," she said. "What will you do about your precious Santana heir?"

Emilio cradled Zac close, holding him securely in the crook of his arm. "Listen to me, my proud, beautiful Grace. The first night I came here you said something to me. When I remembered the words they gave me the courage to come here tonight. What you said was, *There are stronger ties than blood. One of them is love.* Zac will be my son in every way that matters."

His free hand reached out to her, the gesture an unspoken plea. "If you still believe those words, come to me, Grace. I need you in my life. I need Zac. And he needs us both."

Grace's lips moved as she tried to voice a response. But there was nothing more to say. Rising, she took his hand and stepped into the loving circle of his arms.

Epilogue

Two years later

The sleek Gulfstream jet dropped through the clouds and glided onto the runway at Cusco. As the plane taxied to a stop, Grace unbuckled the protective baby seat and lifted her week-old daughter into her arms.

Aching with love, she gazed down at her tiny miracle—conceived in vitro and carried by a healthy surrogate. She would never experience what it was like to give birth. But she'd been in the delivery room to hear her baby's first cry, just as she'd heard Zac's when he was born. It was all she could hope for, and more.

The little girl had Emilio's thick, dark curls. But her eyes and mouth were Grace's, and her imperious little personality was all her own. Her name was Teresa Esperanza, after her two grandmothers. Since *esperanza* also meant hope, her middle name would have special meaning. Grace and Emilio had traveled back and forth to the United States to have the procedures done, the surrogate chosen and the baby delivered. Their first two attempts had ended in disappointment. But at last their daughter was here.

"Are we home now, Papa?" Three-year-old Zac had freed himself from his seat belt and was bounding up and down the aisle. He'd been elated about the new baby and was more than ready to be a big brother. But after the long flight all he wanted was to get back to his friends, his new puppy and the freedom of the estate.

"Almost." Emilio scooped his son to his shoulder as the door of the plane opened and unfolded into steps. "Just another hour in the car. If you can sit still and behave, I'll take you for a ride on Manso tomorrow. We can go fishing at the waterfall. All right?"

"All right!" Zac squirmed with eagerness.

Grace and Emilio had talked about the implications if they were to have another child, especially a boy. On one point, Emilio had been adamant. Adopted or not, Zac was a Santana, the firstborn of the family. His inheritance rights were never to be challenged.

Grace kept one secret thought to herself. Given the changing times and Zac's happy-go-lucky nature, the next jefe of the vast Santana empire just might turn out to be Emilio's strong-willed daughter.

Emilio took her arm to steady her as they stepped out of the plane. Francisco was waiting on the tarmac. A few yards behind him was the car.

"Oh, my goodness!" Grace exclaimed. "Just look at that!"

Flying from a staff on the back of the car was an elaborate pink banner with streamers, ribbons and satin roses.

"I'd say her godmother had a hand in that," Emilio muttered.

"Mercedes will spoil this little girl rotten if we don't draw some lines." Grace chuckled. Her former rival had proven a steadfast friend to her and an adoring honorary aunt to Zac. Now that Mercedes was engaged to a wealthy banker and planning her own wedding, the two women were closer than ever.

As her feet touched the ground of what was now her home country, Grace blinked away a tear and murmured silent thanks to Cassidy. Her stepsister's sacrifice and her gift of Zac had multiplied into more blessings than she'd ever believed possible.

Their family hadn't come together in the usual way. But as Emilio had reminded her, there were ties stronger than blood. One of them was love.

They had love in abundance.

* * * * *

A sneaky peek at next month...

MODERN™

POWER, PASSION AND IRRESISTIBLE TEMPTATION

My wish list for next month's titles...

In stores from 16th May 2014:

❑ Ravelli's Defiant Bride – Lynne Graham

❑ The Heartbreaker Prince – Kim Lawrence

❑ A Question of Honour – Kate Walker

❑ An Heir to Bind Them – Dani Collins

In stores from 6th June 2014:

❑ When Da Silva Breaks the Rules – Abby Green

❑ The Man She Can't Forget – Maggie Cox

❑ What the Greek Can't Resist – Maya Blake

❑ One Night with the Sheikh – Kristi Gold

Available at WHSmith, Tesco, Asda, Eason, Amazon and Apple

Just can't wait?

Visit us Online

You can buy our books online a month before they hit the shops! **www.millsandboon.co.uk**

0514/01

Special Offers

Every month we put together collections and longer reads written by your favourite authors.

Here are some of next month's highlights— and don't miss our fabulous discount online!

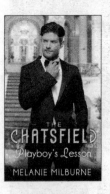

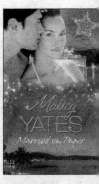

On sale 6th June   On sale 6th June   On sale 6th June

Save 20%
on all Special Releases

Find out more at
www.millsandboon.co.uk/specialreleases

Visit us Online

0614/ST/MB47

THE
CHATSFIELD®

THE CHATSFIELD
Sheikh's Scandal
LUCY MONROE

THE CHATSFIELD
Playboy's Lesson
MELANIE MILBURNE

THE CHATSFIELD
Socialite's Gamble
MICHELLE CONDER

THE CHATSFIELD
Billionaire's Secret
CHANTELLE SHAW

THE CHATSFIELD
Tycoon's Temptation
TRISH MOREY

THE CHATSFIELD
Rival's Challenge
ABBY GREEN

THE CHATSFIELD
Rebel's Bargain
ANNIE WEST

THE CHATSFIELD
Heiress's Defiance
LYNN RAYE HARRIS

Collect all 8!

Buy now at
www.millsandboon.co.uk/thechatsfield

*/MB476

Blaze is now *exclusive* to eBook!

FUN, SEXY AND *ALWAYS STEAMY*!

Our much-loved series about sassy heroines and irresistible heroes are now available exclusively as eBooks. So download yours today and expect sizzling adventures about modern love and lust.

Now available at www.millsandboon.co.uk/blaze

0614/14/MB475

Join our *EXCLUSIVE* eBook club

FROM JUST £1.99 A MONTH!

Never miss a book again with our hassle-free eBook subscription.

★ Pick how many titles you want from each series with our flexible subscription

★ Your titles are delivered to your device on the first of every month

★ Zero risk, zero obligation!

There really is nothing standing in the way of you and your favourite books!

Start your eBook subscription today at www.millsandboon.co.uk/subscribe

OK_SUBS

Join the Mills & Boon Book Club

Subscribe to **Modern**™ today for 3, 6 or 12 months and you could **save over £40!**

We'll also treat you to these fabulous extras:

- 🌹 **FREE L'Occitane gift set worth £10**
- 🌹 **FREE home delivery**
- 🌹 **Rewards scheme, exclusive offers…and much more!**

Subscribe now and save over £40
www.millsandboon.co.uk/subscribeme

SUBS/OFFER/P1